Escape from Krystal

Escape from Krystal

Jenni Lynn

Contents

This is the second book in the Krystal series.

Chapter 1

Narrow Escape

Chief Tyee was sprinting up the mountain, sweat dripping from his forehead and his breathing heavy. Skye was following him as closely as she could, but she was very tired and really scared. She had stumbled a couple of times and was falling behind. Chief Tyee had the precious dragon egg strapped to his chest, trying to keep it warm and safe. He had been protecting it from the thieves for many moons, but the lifters were getting desperate and their attempts to steal the egg were increasing. They were close behind them and were expertly tracking them up the mountain. With the weight of the heavy dragon's egg slowing them down, Chief Tyee was worried that the they were catching up. Chief Tyee wondered whether their fool proof plan was as fool proof as they thought.

"Come on Skye, we are almost to the spot where you can escape to Canada," said Chief Tyee encouragingly.

"I'm trying my hardest, Chief Tyee. You must know that I would do anything, even give up my life for this precious egg," stated Skye defiantly.

"I know you would Skye, that is why I chose you for this mission," said Chief Tyee.

There had not been a golden dragon egg in Krystal for over 100 years. None of the tribe's people had ever even met a dragon from a golden egg. It was rumored, in the old scrolls, that the hatchling from a golden egg was the most powerful of all dragons and that they were almost invincible. Their tribe had already lost two maroon dragon eggs to thieves from another tribe and Chief Tyee had no intention of losing this precious egg. The tired, out of breath pair reached the secret spot on the mountain where they would send Skye through the passage to meet Bella. Zenny, the loving mother of the golden egg, had finally been able to contact Bella yesterday using her powers and the pink crystals. Zenny had arranged for Bella to meet Skye at the other end of the passage between their two worlds. Bella had excitedly agreed to help save the precious dragon egg without a minute's hesitation, just like Chief Tyee had expected. Bella had proven herself such a brave warrior when she had fallen into Krystal, and now she was proving herself again.

Skye was very worried about going to Canada, she knew nothing about the strange land. Would there be trees, grass, beautiful hills and mountains like in her homeland of Krystal? Would the people try to steal their dragon egg when she got there? Would she even make it through the passage? Would there be any food she could eat or cool water to drink? Skye had so many questions and no answers, she just had to be a brave warrior too. Skye realized that they had finally made it to the spot where she and the precious egg were going to enter Canada. She could feel her anxiety begin to grow.

Chief Tyee quickly removed the golden egg from his chest and gave the egg to Skye, "Make sure the straps are secure."

They worked together quickly to secure the precious egg to her chest. "The straps feel really snug and tight. The egg will be safe," said Skye.

Chief Tyee got out the large pink crystals and he began to recite the incantation to activate the passage. The beautiful crystals began to warm and glow in his hands, and the earth began to shift.

"Hurry Chief Tyee, I must get this egg to safety," exclaimed Skye, "This golden egg means so much to our tribe and even more to Zenny and Warrior." Skye had been around the magic of the crystals her whole life, but she was always amazed by Chief Tyee's extraordinary ability to use it. Then suddenly, right before her eyes, he made a passage appear into the mountain with no end in sight. Skye sucked in her breath.

"Okay Skye this is it, hurry through the passage but always guard that egg. Circee will, I mean Bella, will meet you on the other side. Bella's instructions to get through the passage were just to walk through quickly until you see the light and then run toward it. Keep that egg safe at all costs. I will lead the thieves away from the entrance and the portal will close automatically when you are completely through. If Circee, I mean Bella, isn't there yet just wait for her and remember to stay out of sight. She will come," Chief Tyee commanded.

Skye hurried towards the dark entrance, and she was quickly surrounded by the pitch-black darkness of the passage. Her heart began to race, and she was terrified. She cradled the egg with one arm and kept her other arm outstretched to protect the egg from any bumps. Her eyes began to adjust and her excitement built with each step as she hurried through the dark cavern. She kept going faster and faster until she saw the light and as soon as she saw it, she began to run. She ran as fast as she could, guarding the egg carefully in front of her. Her legs began to burn, and her breath was coming in short bursts. She was going to make it!

Chapter 2

Arriving in a New Land

Bella was anxiously waiting at the entrance to Krystal; she had gotten there early in case Skye arrived earlier. She remembered how scary it was to go to a new place alone. The entrance had opened almost five minutes ago, and Bella was still amazed by the magic of Krystal. One minute - rocks and trees, the next - a cavernous passage. She had packed some clothes that she hoped would fit Skye and she had brought some blankets to keep the precious egg warm. Bella had been awake most of the night thinking about Zenny and the egg. She still couldn't believe Zenny was sending her precious dragon egg to her, in Canada of all places, to keep it safe from thieves. A dragon egg in Canada, absolutely no one could find out and Bella herself couldn't even believe it was going to happen.

"I really hope Skye is a girl," Bella chuckled to herself, "or I'm going to have a lot of explaining to do to my mom when I bring them home and ask if they can stay over." Bella thought she heard someone coming and her heart began to race. A couple of minutes later Skye burst through the opening. As quickly as it had appeared, pffft, the opening was gone with just a little dust left behind.

"Hi," Bella said excitedly, "How are you? How's the egg? How's Chief Tyee?"

Skye turned slowly in a circle staring at her new surroundings, as she sucked in a deep breath. "Err, hello. The egg seems fine," stammered Skye. "Maybe a little jostled from our escape. Chief Tyee was fine when I left him, but our enemies were close behind us. I hope he was able to get away, he had some invisibility crystals, and as long as he had time to use them, he will be safe. I'm fine, I think, that was a scary passage. It really helped me, knowing that you had made it safely through it once before. I really didn't want to die in a dark passage all alone. You are very brave Circee, to have been the first to go through that pitch black and unknown passage."

"Thanks," said Bella, "I never really thought of it that way, I just really wanted to get home. Can you please call me Bella here because that's my name in Canada? I don't want to attract any unnecessary attention."

"Oh, sorry Circee, I mean Bella. I'm so sorry," said Skye as both girls began to laugh. Bella looked appraisingly at Skye and her unusual clothes.

"Let's get you changed into some of my clothes so you can fit in better in Canada. Your clothes are a little bit different than what we're used to here," said Bella. Skye looked down at the clothes she was wearing, leather pants and a leather shirt and the moccasins she had made herself. "Don't get me wrong, your clothes are very beautiful, but we need to have you blend in to keep you and the egg safe. I'm also really glad you're a girl Skye, it will make explaining you so much easier to my Mom. We can even share my clothes and my bedroom at my house."

Skye smiled and began unhooking the straps that held the heavy egg. Bella got the blankets ready that she had brought to keep the egg warm, and the girls laid the egg very carefully into the makeshift nest. After the girls got the egg settled, Bella went and got the clothes she had brought and gave them to Skye. She had brought Skye some pants and a t-shirt. She made sure the pants were sweatpants so they would be easier to fit into, even if Skye was a different size than Bella. Skye changed quickly while Bella stood guard holding up one of the blankets as a makeshift change room.

"How do I look?" asked Skye as they hid her clothes in the backpack Bella had brought.

"You look very Canadian," laughed Bella." I'm so glad my clothes fit. I had been a bit worried you might be extra tall and then my clothes wouldn't have looked good. We should hurry now and get going." The girls carefully carried the precious egg over to Bella's car. Skye was looking around and couldn't believe all the things she was seeing. The tall trees, the big lake, and suddenly so many people. It hadn't been a long walk from the entrance to Krystal to where they were, but Skye couldn't believe the changes she was seeing all around her. It really was a new world.

"Skye, there's my car over there," said Bella, pointing at a small red car.

"Your car is very pretty Bella, it's the color of apples when they are ready to be picked," said Skye admiringly. When they got to Bella's car Skye was scared to get in. "I am a little fearful of your car," said Skye, "I have never seen anything like it before."

"That's to be expected," said Bella. "I felt the same way when I landed in Krystal. Everything was new and different. Canada will take some getting used to. I can tell you that riding in a car is a little like riding a dragon, fast and sometimes scary. Fortunately, you will have the advantage of a seat belt to hold you in," chuckled Bella. "Warrior didn't have a seat belt when I fell into Krystal."

Skye looked at the car unsure how to get in. Bella smiled and pulled up the handle and opened the door. Skye got into the car and sat for a minute to get used to the strange seat. "Bella, Are you sure about this?" she asked.

Bella laughed, "I've only been driving for a little over a year but I'm doing pretty well, you'll be fine." Skye settled herself deeper into the front seat and put on her seat belt the way Bella had instructed her.

"This seat is very comfortable Bella, are all cars like this?" asked Skye.

"All cars have seats, but most cars are bigger than this one. This is a very compact car," laughed Bella. "OK, let's get this egg safely to my house." Bella settled the beautiful golden egg onto Skye's lap. Bella went around and got into the driver's seat and put the keys in the ignition. "Well Skye, are you ready to go?"

"I guess so Bella, this day has certainly been a big adventure," said Skye.

"Oh, the adventures are going to get bigger, Skye. Let's go have some fun." Bella turned the keys in the ignition and her little car roared to life. Skye jumped in her seat. Thank goodness for seat belts or she may have toppled the egg.

"What's that noise?" asked Skye fearfully. Bella laughed.

"It's just the engine Skye, that's what helps the car to move," said Bella. Bella gently put the car in gear and began their drive home. There were many sights along the way. The first sight Bella showed Skye was a golf course. Skye had never seen golf before.

"I can't believe that people walk around and hit a ball into a far-off hole just for fun. Wouldn't shooting arrows be more practical?" she asked. Bella just smiled. Skye was even more surprised when they drove a little further and there was a herd of cows in a field. "Do those large animals just stay behind that small, thin blockade? "asked Skye.

"Those are dairy cows and they do stay in their fields most of the time, once in a while one might make an escape," said Bella. "The farmers milk them and use their milk to make lots of different types of food, like ice cream, cheese, and butter."

"I have never seen so many large animals in the same field before. Why are most of them just black and white?"

"That's a special type of cow called a Holstein, they're what's used by the dairy farmers to get the most milk. There are a lot of people in Canada and so we need to have a lot of milk cows to help feed everyone." A gravel truck drove past the girls and Skye jumped again!

"What was that?" exclaimed Skye.

"That was a double pup gravel truck, it carries rocks to help fix our roads," said Bella.

"Oh Bella, this Canada place sure is different from Krystal," said Skye.

"I hope that you enjoy your stay here with me. I have lots of fun things planned for us to do. I'll even ask mom if I can take you to the mall, it's one of the biggest malls in Canada," said Bella.

"What's a mall?" asked Skye.

"A mall is where shops are all grouped together in one place, and you can buy almost anything you can imagine," Bella's eyes lit up as she answered.

"Wow Bella, I've never imagined anything like Canada so I'm sure it will be very exciting to go to the mall," said Skye. The girls drove for about half an hour more before they arrived at Bella's house.

"So, what did you think of the car ride Skye?" asked Bella when she was helping her get the egg out of the car.

"It was a little scary in parts, especially when the huge gravel car passed us, but I think that you are a very good driver. I also really enjoyed seeing the countryside, there are so many cars and people here it seems very busy compared to Krystal. I know almost everyone at home, it would be impossible to know all these people," said Skye.

"That's for sure Skye, I barely know my neighbors let alone everyone in the city. Let's head into the house," said Bella, "and you can meet someone I do know, my awesome Mom."

"Do I look okay to meet your Mom?" asked Skye, "I sure hope that we can keep our secret and not let it slip out about the dragon egg."

"We're going to take the dragon's egg up to my room and find it a safe hiding spot until it's time for you to take it back to Krystal." The two girls went into the house and upstairs to Bella's room to find a nice warm hiding place for Zenny's golden egg. The girls checked under the bed but that wasn't right. They checked in the closet but that wasn't right either. Then Bella had an idea - she dumped out her laundry and settled the egg into the laundry basket with the blankets the girls had wrapped it in. Then, she put the basket into the closet along with her laundry.

"That looks perfect," said the girls together. "No one will suspect anything."

Chapter 3

Deadly enemies.

ack in Krystal, Chief Tyee was anxiously praying that the passage would close quickly so that he could make his escape. Just as he was losing all hope that his escape would happen, the passageway suddenly shifted and disappeared. Relief flooded Chief Tyee; Skye had made it! He could hear his enemies closing in they were very close. He knew he would have to use the orange disappearing crystals if he was going to escape. He was hoping he had enough strength to get the crystals to help him levitate as well. He quickly retrieved the crystals from his waist pouch and felt them begin to warm in his hands; he summoned more strength, and they began to glow. He could hear the thieves getting closer; they were almost upon him. Their heavy footsteps moved steadily in his direction. There must be a large group of them, judging from the amount of noise they were making. He felt the crystals heating even more and watched his legs as they disappeared. He felt himself becoming weightless as he began to rise. A minute later the thieves were beside him, he could see the faces of the men who had been tracking him. He held his breath until they had passed his location.

These men were strangers to him; they were too big to be from the tribe that had been trying to steal the life crystal. What tribe could they be from, or even what world? Chief Tyee had often worried that if he could send Bella back to another world maybe people from the other world could come in to his. Once the thieves had passed, he put one orange crystal in his pocket so he could lower himself back to the ground, but he continued to hold the other crystal, so he would remain invisible. It took a lot of his energy to use the magic from the crystals and he was very tired. He quickly had a drink of his water and proceeded back down the mountain. He went back the way the thieves had come from, because he was hoping to find some clues as to who they were and why they were trying so desperately to steal their dragon eggs.

Chief Tyee didn't find anything of value at first, just a very beaten down trail and broken tree branches. He had been walking about a half mile when he finally discovered something useful. He had been looking up at the trees when he saw it, a broken arrow embedded in the bark of a big buckeye tree. He would have to climb up to get the arrow. He carefully tucked the orange crystals back in his pouch so his hands would be free to climb and watched in awe as his legs and arms quickly became visible again. Magic is amazing! He needed to climb up two enormous branches to be able to reach the arrow. It took most of his remaining strength to dislodge the arrow from its mark in the towering buckeye tree. When Chief Tyee finally got the arrow free, he let out a low whistle. The shaft of the arrow was wood, and the bird feathers used for flight were similar to his own arrows, but this arrow had a very peculiar tip. The tip wasn't made from stone like he was used to; it was made from something darker and very hard. This arrow also had jagged edges, that is why it had been so hard to remove from the tree. The tip looked a bit like the fork Circee had made when she was practicing how to use the green transformation crystals. What was this strange arrow tip made from, and even more importantly what tribe made it?

The chief decided he would send for Bade as soon as he arrived home and he would also ask his sister to start researching in the ancient scrolls about the far away tribes. Together they would try to find out who these dangerous thieves may be. Chief Tyee found another broken arrow in the trees; this one had the same dark tip but very different bird feathers. The feathers were all white and there were colorful markings on the wooden shaft. He hoped this would be a big enough clue to help discover their enemy's identity.

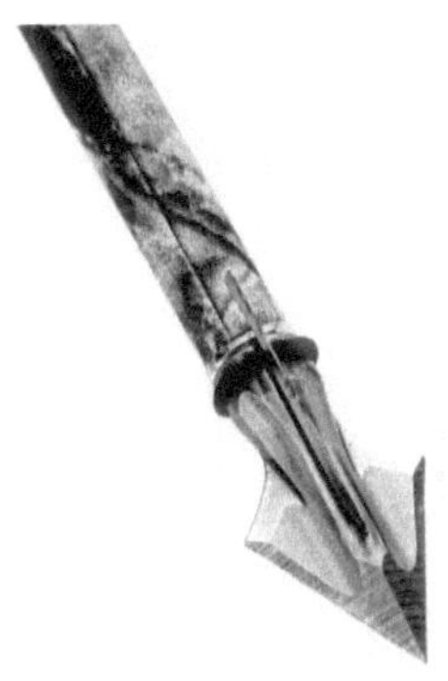

Chapter 4

Getting Home

Chief Tyee was exhausted from his day but couldn't stop to rest, he had to get home. He had finished the last of his water after climbing the Buckeye tree and his throat was now feeling dry and scratchy. "Just a few more miles," he thought to himself, "You can make it." Suddenly, he caught sight of the magnificent Warrior walking quickly towards him to bring him home. Chief Tyee had never been so happy to see his dragon. "Warrior, I am so glad to see you. Thank you for coming and for obeying the no-fly rule," said Chief Tyee as he collapsed onto Warrior's back.

"I have been very worried about you, Skye, and my precious egg. I see you are alone so that must mean Skye made it safely through the passage to Canada," Warrior communicated to Chief Tyee as he started the long walk home with him on his back.

"Yes, she made it through, and the passage closed just minutes before the thieves were upon me. I had to use the orange crystals to disappear and levitate or they would have caught me. I was just a few feet away from them. I could see their faces and smell their stench," exclaimed Chief Tyee.

"You are very brave my friend, thank you for protecting my egg," communicated Warrior gratefully.

"I would do anything for you, and that egg means so much, not only to you but to our whole tribe," expressed Chief Tyee.

They walked in companionable silence the rest of the way home. Chief Tyee gratefully rested on Warrior's back. His legs and arms were so tired his muscles were twitching uncomfortably. "Can you take me to get water from the Well of Truth when we get home? It is the most refreshing water and I think my body could use some of that to replenish my exhausted muscles," Chief Tyee requested.

"Anything you wish," communicated Warrior, "I see someone else who couldn't wait for you to get home." Warrior communicated to Chief Tyee with a snort. Chief Tyee sat up to look and saw the magnificent Zenny approaching them. "Everything is well Zenny, Skye made it through the passage to Canada with our precious baby and our brave Chief Tyee has made it back to us. He is very exhausted and so I am taking him to get water from the Well of Truth," communicated Warrior to Zenny.

"I'm so glad that everyone is safe, I have been very worried. Did our plan work? Did Chief Tyee and Skye get away without being followed by the thieves?" Zenny asked.

"No, the thieves managed to track them somehow and almost caught Chief Tyee while he was waiting for the passageway to close. That is why he is so tired, he had to use a lot of crystal magic just to escape."

"I'm very glad he made it and I'm also thankful that we have such a brave Chief. You two go to the back and get some water, and I will get Alli to come out and help him get into the house. He seems so weak," said Zenny.

Warrior went around the house and over to the Well of Truth. Chief Tyee slowly struggled to slide off Warrior's back. Warrior supported him at the fountain so he could drink his fill and fill his water bottle with the thirst-quenching water. Zenny had banged on the side door with her talons and managed to get Chief Tyee's sister, Alli's, attention and they both came back hurrying around the side of the house.

"Tyee my brother, are you hurt?" she called as she ran to his side. "Warrior, can you go quickly and get Bade?" Warrior started to hurry as fast as he could towards Bade's house, careful to still obey the no-fly rule.

"No, my sister, I am not injured but I needed to use a lot of crystal magic to open the passageway, and to become invisible and levitate to avoid capture. I also ran for many miles up a mountain carrying a very heavy healthy golden dragon egg," Chief Tyee chuckled, "My muscles are protesting a bit, can you please help me into the house?" Chief Tyee asked tiredly. His sister supported him with his arm over her shoulder and her arm around his waist. Chief Tyee leaned heavily against her as they walked toward the door. Zenny had gone ahead of them and pushed the door open so they could get into the house. She then stood guard at the entrance until Chief Tyee was safely laying on the couch.

"Tyee what is all this about the passageway and thieves and Warrior's egg? What have you done, and why didn't you tell anyone?" demanded his sister. Chief Tyee still had the arrows clutched in his left hand and he slowly uncurled his cramping fingers and handed them to his sister. "What are these broken arrows? Are they from the dragon thieves? Judging from all these jagged edges, whoever made this arrow tip is very serious about killing," Alli emphasized by waving the arrow around. "Now what have you been up to?"

"Warrior, Zenny, and I came up with what we thought was an ingenious plan to get the precious egg out of Krystal. As it turned out it wasn't so fool proof as we had thought it would be, the thieves were on our trail before we even made it to the mountain."

Just then Bade burst through the door, he was out of breath and had his sword drawn for a fight. "Where are they? I will cut them to ribbons!" yelled Bade. "Are you hurt my love?"

"No, I am not injured, I am perfectly fine, my brave man," smiled Alli.

"I am fine too," laughed Chief Tyee, "thanks for 'not' asking."

"Warrior was running. I thought something must be wrong. I grabbed my sword and ran as fast as I could to try and help," Bade explained as he collapsed into a chair beside the couch. Alli came over and kissed him lovingly on the forehead. Bade and Alli had been dating for years and had recently become betrothed.

"You are a wonderful man and a very brave warrior. I love you," said Alli with a big smile on her face. Bade smiled lovingly back at her.

"Can someone please tell me what is going on and why Tyee looks like he's seen better days?" Bade inquired accusingly.

"Tyee was just getting to that, please wait with the telling of the story until I get back with some food and warm cocoa for all of us. I think this story might take a while and Tyee needs some food and drink, so he can gain enough energy to tell it. Here, look at these while I'm gone," said Alli, as she handed the arrows to Bade and left the room to get some food. Bade's face paled as he looked at the arrows.

"What are you thinking my friend? I can tell by that face that the arrows made you think of something," stated Chief Tyee.

Chapter 5

Ruthless Neighbors

"The white feathers remind me of an old story my dad used to tell me about a tribe in the deep south who have these giant white birds that can grow to be three or four feet tall with a wingspan of over six feet. He called them giant egrets. The birds are huge and daunting, but they are not the problem, it's the tribe who lives by them that is of the greatest concern. The people who hunt these birds are ruthless and will hunt just to kill instead of for food. I hope that is not who we are dealing with," sighed Bade.

"They were large and smelly men; they had been away from home for at least a fortnight judging by the length of their beards. They were carrying their packs, so they didn't appear to be close to their camp. Also, the missing   dragon eggs couldn't have fit into their packs as they were too small, so they must have taken the eggs home. That or we are dealing with more than one group. My preliminary assessment of that barbed arrow makes me think that they are pretty serious hunters," informed Chief Tyee.

"Those are very good observations my friend, their putrid smell will make it easier for the dragons to track them and their size will make it easier for us to hit them with our weapons. I will start practicing again with the green crystals and maybe I can transform them into mice like the Brave Circee did to our past enemies," declared Bade. Alli returned with a tray laden with food and warm cocoa for the three of them.

"Thank you Alli, this is just what I needed," Chief Tyee said as he picked up a muffin from the tray. Bade grabbed a bun filled with meat and his mug of warm cocoa.

"Thank you Alli, you are always just what I need," Bade smiled as he spoke.

Alli laughed as she reached for her mug of cocoa and then sat in a chair between the two powerful men. "So, what were you discussing? Please fill me in."

"Tyee was telling me about the very large smelly men he saw…"

"…and Bade was telling me about a story his Dad used to tell him," interrupted Chief Tyee.

"I have heard a bit about these large aromatic men, so please tell me about the story your father told and how it relates to the smelly men," laughed Alli.

"When I was little, he used to tell me stories about these huge birds called giant egrets. They are all white and they live in the deep south close to a tribe of large fierce hunters who hunt without conscience. My father described the tribe as ruthless and barbaric in the stories, but I don't know if the stories were embellished for a small boy or if they were fact," stated Bade.

"I think we should find the scrolls about the different tribes and try to learn as much as we can about this particular tribe. They most likely won't have the same ruler that was alive when the scrolls were written, but at least we will know more about where they are from and possibly learn why they are so desperately trying to steal our dragons' eggs," advised Alli.

"That's just what I was thinking, you must have read my mind," Chief Tyee laughed. "I am also very glad that you are so talented at finding things in the ancient scrolls. I really should have paid better attention to the scrolls in school," acknowledged Chief Tyee.

"Alli, can you get the scrolls, and start looking through them for information about our enemies and I will go get a search party together. After you have slept, Tyee, we will go in search of our enemies," Bade explained.

"I will get the scrolls and start searching for information on this southern tribe, hopefully I will have more information for you when you return. I will look for clues that will be useful in tracking them and hopefully defeating them quickly. We must keep our dragons safe from these violent people," insisted Alli.

"Yes, we must protect our dragons and our tribe at all costs," said Bade. "I will meet you back here in a couple of hours to go through the ancient scrolls and I will have the tracking party organized to leave from the clearing at dawn." Bade gave Alli a kiss as he was leaving, and they both began to chuckle as they heard a loud snore coming from the couch. Chief Tyee was already asleep; he was so exhausted from his brave mission to save the egg.

Alli closed and locked the door after Bade left and headed to the basement to look for the ancient scrolls that contained information about the other tribes. One hour turned into two and she was still searching through the ancient scrolls and had only found a few scrolls that even mentioned the other tribes. She took these scrolls up and laid them on the table. Tyee was, without a doubt, still sleeping on the couch as there was still loud snoring coming from his direction. Alli sat down and picked up the scroll closest to her and began to read. This scroll was all about the small tribe they had just defeated over their life crystal. She put that scroll aside and reached for the next. Alli heard a knock at the door and ran to open it for Bade. He smiled and embraced her, "How's the most beautiful girl in the world?"

Alli blushed and gave him an extra kiss. "I am better now that you are here, I haven't found the right scroll yet, but I have found several for us to start searching through. I really hope we find some information about this southern tribe that will help us defeat them," Alli passed a scroll to Bade before asking, "How did it go getting the tracking party together?"

"I have arranged four tracking parties and we plan to meet in the clearing at dawn. We will be able to travel in every direction to find clues to the whereabouts of our enemies and then we can determine how to drive them from our land and recover our stolen dragon eggs," exclaimed Bade.

"That is great news to wake up to," affirmed a sleepy Chief Tyee as he stretched on the couch.

"Brother, I'm so glad you are awake. How are you feeling?" asked Alli anxiously.

"I'm feeling much encouraged after hearing Bade's news that he was able to raise not just one, but four tracking parties from our brave tribe. How did you manage with the scrolls Alli? We are going to need all the information we can gather to gain the advantage against these ruthless people," stated Chief Tyee.

"I have found a few scrolls that have made mention of some of the other tribes, and I was just starting to read through them to try and find information on the southernmost tribe. I have them here on the table maybe we could read through them together?" suggested Alli.

"That sounds great, could I talk you into making us some food too please? I woke up very hungry," Chief Tyee asked hopefully.

"I haven't eaten either," stated Bade, "I will help you get a meal ready Alli, if that's agreeable to you? Tyee, you can sit down and get a head start reading the scrolls."

"I would love your help making a meal for the three of us," said Alli with a smile as she walked toward the kitchen.

Chief Tyee slowly sat up and stretched again. Then with a loud groan he stood on his aching legs and walked over to where the scrolls were waiting for him.

"Alli, I thought you said you didn't find many scrolls; this is a huge pile. How will I ever get through all of these?" Chief Tyee sighed as he picked up his first scroll.

"No complaining allowed," laughed Alli. "I really wish I had found more but this will give us a place to start at least. You will have more energy for reading once we've eaten some food." Alli and Bade worked together seamlessly to prepare a delicious meal for the three of them. Bade focussed on making the Macaluba and Alli got some vegetables and drinks ready. The two were even able to quickly prepare a sweet dessert for after the meal.

Chief Tyee was just starting his second scroll when Bade and Alli entered with steaming trays of wonderful smelling food. Chief Tyee inhaled deeply, "That smells amazing you two, thank you both."

"Did you find anything of interest in the scrolls while we were slaving away making this meal?" inquired Bade.

"No such luck, I was just going to start my second scroll but there was no mention of the southern tribe in my first," the Chief answered.

"Let's eat our food before it gets cold and then we will keep reading. I'm sure we will find something of value in one of these old scrolls," said Alli as she set down her tray at the end of the table and passed Chief Tyee his plate of Macaluba.

"What an appropriate dish, Circee's favorite. That girl sure could eat." Chief Tyee smiled at his memory of Circee.

"I thought every food was her favorite when I watched her eat, her appetite was second to none," Bade recalled, remembering Circee fondly.

"I wish she was here; she could turn our enemies into mice and then they would return our dragon eggs and go back to their own land," Alli said as she began eating her Macaluba.

"When I was locked in the cage of our enemies, scared for my life and Bella Circee came riding in on Zenny and was turning my captors into mice I couldn't believe how brave she was. I also couldn't believe how happy I was to see her." remembered Bade with a smile.

"She was brave, and she worked tirelessly to save our people and our purple life crystal. Circee and Zenny made such a magnificent team," Alli added.

"I am glad she is helping Skye guard the precious golden egg; I know we can trust her to keep it safe. She truly cares for Zenny and would do anything for her," said Chief Tyee confidently. The three continued their meal, Chief Tyee had double portions of everything. "Maybe all this Macaluba will give me some extra courage, it seemed to work for Circee."

"This was a wonderful meal. I hope it did come complete with a helping of extra courage, I might need some tomorrow if I find our enemies," said Bade.

"Let's get back to reading the scrolls now," said Chief Tyee as he put his dishes on the tray at the end of the table and picked up the second scroll that he had just started to read before the meal had arrived. Bade got up and cleared the trays from the table as Alli picked up a large scroll to start searching for important clues about the southern tribe. Alli and Chief Tyee were each deep into reading their scrolls when Bade returned with warm cocoa for everyone.

"This will help us burn the midnight oil and get through all of these scrolls," said Bade with a grin as he passed around the three large mugs.

Chapter 6

Warm Memories

"You definitely love your warm cocoa," laughed Chief Tyee as he looked at Bade. "I remember as kids you would say you were cold just to get your kind Mom to make you some."

"Yes, and she would always give me a chore to do while she made it, so it was a victory for both of us. She was a wise woman," reminisced Bade.

"Your mother did make great warm cocoa. She sometimes added a secret ingredient that would make it even better," said Alli.

"She sure did, in the warm months she would add a little vanilla or cinnamon but in the cold months she would add cayenne, so it was double warm cocoa," remembered Bade fondly.

"I remember my whole mouth burning from your mom's cocoa. I thought I had just taken too big of a drink, but the cayenne explains it," laughed Chief Tyee.

"Come on you two, we had better get back to business reading these scrolls," said Alli determinedly.

"You are right as always my dear," smiled Bade as he picked up a large scroll and started unrolling it gently.

The three of them read intently for over an hour when Alli let out a squeal. "I found the first reference to the southern tribe; it says they fought over the location of the tribe's home and the tribe had a violent war. They divided and some of them went into the deep south over two hundred years ago looking for more fertile farmlands and larger amounts of wild game to hunt," said Alli.

"If they were farmers and hunters like we are, where did my father hear the violent stories?" Bade asked.

"It sounds like the ones who left to the deep south were unhappy with just farming and that's why they separated. Any people that would fight and kill their own neighbors are certainly worth being concerned about. Does it say anything else about the southernmost tribe in that scroll, Alli?" asked Chief Tyee.

"I will keep reading and if anything comes up, I will be the first to let you know," said Alli with a grin. The three continued their reading in hopes of discovering something useful to help defeat this enemy tribe. "Nothing else in this scroll," said Alli as she reached for a new scroll to start searching through.

"I'm not having any luck in this scroll either, I am going to go check on Warrior and the other dragons. I will be back in less than an hour," Chief Tyee stated as he strode frustratedly to the back door on his way to the dragon's keep.

"Okay see you later," called Alli as Chief Tyee left. Alli and Bade smiled happily at each other as they kept reading the scrolls. It was over an hour later when Chief Tyee came back to the house. "Welcome back Tyee. How is everyone in the keep? Is Zenny doing okay or is she worrying about her egg?" asked Alli.

"Hi, sorry I took so long I was talking to Warrior and Zenny. They are both doing as well as can be expected. They are worried about the egg, but they trust Skye and Circee, or should I say Bella? I can only think of Bella as the brave Goddess Circee, it's hard to think of her as plain Bella after all she did for our people and especially our family," Chief Tyee's voice held great admiration for Circee.

"I agree with you, I will be forever grateful to her for saving my life and the life of my beautiful wife-to-be," said Bade as he reached for Alli's hand. Chief Tyee reached for another scroll and hoped they would soon find the information that would help defeat their enemies.

"Finally", whispered Alli, "I think I have found something, but it's not sounding very good for us. This southern tribe is described as a murderous and uncaring lot. The scroll starts with a retelling of how they murdered the leader of their tribe and his whole family including an infant son. They also stole their tribe's savings when they separated from the main tribe and then disappeared into the deep south. The stories of lootings and killings continue until the end of this scroll," Chief Tyee looked at Alli with a somber expression.

"We are going to need to be on high alert and we can not go anywhere alone with these ruthless enemies in our midst. I am very grateful to have made it back alive from my adventure," said Chief Tyee solemnly.

"It seems that these people have no honour and are very dangerous," Bade added. "I'm very glad you implemented the no-fly rule for our dragons, it sounds like they wouldn't hesitate to harm one."

"I'm so scared for the two eggs they have stolen. Can you imagine being raised with such ruthless people? What if the hatchlings don't even live because they don't know what to watch for when they start to hatch or what they need for their first feeding? What if the baby connects with someone in their tribe before we can successfully retrieve them?" Alli's voice shook with great concern.

The three friends sat in silence thinking about what might happen to the baby dragons if they weren't recovered and what they may need to deal with in the coming days. They kept reading and searching the scrolls in hopes of finding some clue to a weakness, or something that would make the other tribe vulnerable. Maybe something that could give them an advantage or at the very least a fighting chance.

"I've found it," shouted Bade, "this scroll says that they are great hunters and that their marksmanship is second to none."

"How is that helping," groaned Chief Tyee, "that sounds like it's actually making it worse."

"No, it keeps going and says that they are very superstitious and believe in dark magic. If we could turn a couple of their men into mice like the great Circee did in our last battle, I think it would be enough to send them all scurrying back to the deep south. No pun intended," laughed Bade. The others laughed with him.

"What do you two think we should focus on, teaching our warriors how to use the green transformation crystals, or just having a couple of us practice with them?" asked Chief Tyee.

"I think our crystals need to be guarded carefully especially from ruthless people like these, so I think just two or three using the crystals would be ideal," said Alli.

"I agree. We need to keep the crystals safe from these enemies. I will practice with the green crystals. Tyee, you are already skilled with the crystals, and Zenny was able to use them in the last battle. We would have to train her rider though," Bade added.

"If Zenny agrees, I will be her rider," declared Alli. "I will practice nonstop to master the use of the green crystals."

"I think Zenny will happily agree to that," said Chief Tyee, "I'm glad to have you aboard this time. Tomorrow you and I can go and get new green crystals from the cavern that you found; we will take Warrior with us for an extra guard. Bade, could you coordinate the search parties in the morning on your own, and then wait for them to report back to you with their findings? We can plan our next move after that."

"That sounds like a great plan," said Bade agreeably. "Please be extra careful on your journey to get the crystals. It is a very far distance to travel without a dragon to fly on. You two can also be the scouts that way and look for any signs of the invading tribe."

"I think we have everything settled, so I am going to go catch up on my beauty sleep. Bade, you can stay here in the spare room if you like. It's better not to be alone in your home. Goodnight you two," said Chief Tyee.

"Thank you, I will accept that kind offer. Dawn will come very quickly."

"Goodnight Tyee. I will be ready to go first thing in the morning to collect the new crystals," said Alli.

Chief Tyee walked slowly to his bedroom after stopping for a glass of water. He closed his large wooden bedroom door behind him with a thump. Alli and Bade sat together lovingly, talking about their plans for the coming day.

Chapter 7

BIG adjustments

Bella smiled at her new friend. "Now that the egg is settled, are you hungry Skye?" asked Bella.

"I am quite hungry, but I'm a little worried that there won't be any food that I can eat here," Skye answered.

"Our food does look different than what you have in Krystal, but I'm sure that we can find something that you'll like. My first meal when I crash landed in Krystal was Macaluba. We have something very similar to that here and even though it looks very different it tastes almost the same. Let's head down to the kitchen and I will make you some macaroni with cheese." The two girls went down to the kitchen. Bella opened the cupboard, got out a pot, filled it with water and put it on the stove to boil.

"How does that cook your food; where's the fire?" asked Skye.

"Bella laughed; our stove is electric, so it doesn't have fire, but it does get very hot so be careful. Don't touch it by accident."

"How does it get hot without fire?" asked Skye.

"That is a very long story, but it's called electricity and it not only heats our stove, but it also keeps our food cool in the fridge, and it does about a million other things." Bella gently stirred the bubbling pot, after a few minutes the macaroni looked cooked. Bella drained the macaroni and ripped open the cheese packet. Bella's mom came in the back door just as Bella was putting the cheese and butter into the macaroni. "Hi Mom," said Bella, "this is my friend Skye."

"Hello Skye, it's nice to meet you. I was just out working in the garden. If you girls are looking for something to do, there are some weeds that would love you to pull them out," Mom chuckled.

"Hello, it is very nice to meet you too," said Skye, "I would love to help in the garden."

"Sure Mom, we can help later. I'm just making some mac and cheese for us. Hey, I was wondering if Skye could stay for the weekend. I was hoping I could take her to the mall. Skye has never been, and I think she would really like it."

"You've never been to the mall!" exclaimed Bella's Mom. "Of course, she can stay, if it's alright with her family, and you can definitely take her to the mall. Enjoy your lunch girls. I'll see you later in the garden." Bella's Mom left the kitchen through the back door humming an old song.

Bella scooped the mac and cheese into bowls and added some grated cheese on the top. Skye was watching Bella closely as she handed her the bowl of bright orange stuff and a funny looking silver spoon. Skye was especially curious about the spoon.

"I have never seen a spoon like this before. It is very strange; our spoons are made from dark stone. What is this bowl made from? It feels like stone, but it doesn't look like stone?" queried Skye.

"It's a type of glass, many things here are made from glass."

"We have glass in Krystal, but you can see through it. We don't make bowls from it, they would just break," Skye laughed. "This macaroni does smell good, and my stomach is talking to me, so I guess I'm going to give it a try." Skye put the first bite of macaroni and cheese up to her nose, "This smells really good too Bella. Thank you!"

As Skye put the macaroni and cheese into her mouth, Bella watched her reaction and began to smile. "So, what do you think?" she asked Skye.

Skye finished chewing and said, "This is scrumptious Bella, and you are right it tastes a lot like macaluba." The two girls hungrily finished their Mac and cheese.

"Are you thirsty?" asked Bella.

"I would love a drink of water," said Skye. Bella grabbed a couple of water bottles from the fridge, and they headed upstairs to check on the egg.

"Tell me more about this amazing egg, what are we watching for and when will we know it's time to send you home so that it can hatch in Krystal with Zenny?" asked Bella with interest.

"Chief Tyee has had me working in the Dragon's keep for the last two years. I love to hang out with the Dragons and help look after them. When the little ones are about to hatch, I keep them close to their mothers and help out in any way that I can. I am also an expert at making hatchling rations based on the size of the new baby. If this special egg is like the other dragon eggs, then it will begin to flash about two days before it is ready to hatch. We will need to keep a close eye on it, and when we notice it flashing, we will have some time to contact Chief Tyee and get it back to Krystal before the baby hatches," explained Skye.

"Alright. So how many days do you think we have until the egg starts to flash?" asked Bella.

"We only have two or three days until we see the flashing and then we will have to quickly make plans for my return. I'm a little scared to go back through the passageway. What if I fall like you did into the big blue sky; the egg could get hurt?" asked Skye worriedly.

"When I fell into Krystal there had been an actual earthquake here in Canada and the ground just opened and I fell straight through to your world. I was exceptionally lucky that Warrior had sensed I was coming and caught me in mid-air. When we send you back, we're going to open the passageway, so I think you'll just be able to walk back, or run, just like you did when you came here." explained Bella reassuringly.

"Okay," said Skye, "I just have to trust you guys and believe that this is all going to work out. My only mission is to get this beautiful egg back to Krystal in one piece."

"Tell me more about Zenny and Warrior and how this egg came to be," Bella inquired with a smile.

"Oh yes, what a wonderful story that is! One for the history scrolls for sure. After you left, Zenny and Warrior became even closer friends than they had been before. Warrior was so proud of how you and Zenny had acted in the battles to save our crystals that he spent considerably more time with Zenny and seemed to be kind of looking after her. He would let her eat first and they would always fly together. I don't know for sure about dragons, but it seems like they fell in love. This beautiful golden egg is the result of their mating. Zenny and Warrior both love this egg very much. It will be their first baby together and it is Warriors first baby ever. Zenny has other children, but their father was killed over 20 years ago when he saved some hatchlings from a lightning strike. Zenny hasn't had any eggs since then until this amazing egg with Warrior. Isn't that romantic?" sighed Skye.

"That is a very sweet story. I'm so happy for Zenny, she is a fantastic dragon, and she is my good friend. Zenny protected me during the battles to save the crystals and she always had my back and looked out for me. I tried my best to protect her too."

"Zenny has told me stories about the great battles. She said that you were the bravest person she had ever met, and she couldn't believe you actually turned our enemies' soldiers into mice with the magic crystals. Zenny was so glad that she was able to connect with you. I have connected with Zenny too. There's only a select few of us that Zenny can talk with, Chief Tyee communicates through Warrior to Zenny. There was a lot of discussion about how we would be able to keep this beautiful egg safe. Zenny was really worried about her egg going to Canada, but she knew you would protect her baby at all costs," stated Skye.

"I will definitely do everything I can to guard Zenny's precious baby," Bella stated confidently.

Skye glanced out the window, "Are you ready to head out to the garden now? I think your mom would really appreciate our help."

"Sure thing," said Bella, "Let's go." The two girls closed up the closet and headed back downstairs and out the back door to the garden to help Bella's mom with the weeds.

Chapter 8

The unwelcome visitor

Mom stood up and smiled when the girls came through the back door. "Welcome girls! I'm very glad you are here, let's get you two started on this never-ending job of weeding," said Mom. Bella smiled at her Mom she knew how much her Mom loved the garden and how proud she was of it.

Bella got started weeding a row of carrots because they were so hard to tell the difference between weeds and the little plants. Mum showed Skye how to weed the potatoes because it was easier to see the difference between the bigger potato leaves and the weeds. Skye was happy to be learning all about the plants and the weeds. Bella's mom was more than happy to share her knowledge with someone that had such a great interest. Mom taught Skye about pigweed, stinging nettles, and chickweed. Bella was tired of weeding after about half an hour, but Skye was still having so much fun that it was even fun for Bella to watch her while she slowly continued weeding the next row of carrots.

As they were working, they heard the doorbell ringing and ringing as well as someone pounding on the door.

"That is weird, no one knocks like that. Who could it be? You girls go upstairs, and I will answer the door." The girls hurried to Bella's bedroom and checked the egg. It was safe and warm in the laundry basket.

"What's going on?" Skye asked, "is there any danger for us or the egg?"

"I don't think so, but Mom will let us know after she talks to whoever is impatiently at the door," said Bella. The girls sat quietly in Bella's room and waited for Mom. They could hear muffled voices but couldn't make out the words. Finally, they heard the door close. Mom came up the stairs and into the bedroom. "Who was that Mom?" Bella asked anxiously.

"That was the overzealous seismic scientist from the University. You remember him, he showed up when you came home after the earthquake. Girls, is there something you need to tell me?" asked Bella's mom accusingly. Bella's mom was standing with her hands on her hips and a solemn expression on her face. Bella and Skye both looked guiltily at the floor and Skye began to fidget nervously with her hands.

"I never thought we would see him again," said Bella anxiously. "What did he say Mom?"

"He said that they picked up the same frequency of earthquake that happened after you came home last time. He also said it was at the same approximate location as last time. He was very insistent that he needs to talk to you about it. Why do you think that is?" Mom questioned with raised eyebrows.

"Mom, you better sit down," said Bella.

"Oh my, that's not a good sign," chuckled Mom as she sat down on the edge of Bella's bed. The girls sheepishly began to tell the story.

"It all started two days ago when Zenny contacted me with the pink crystals. You know, the ones that I hide at the back of my underwear drawer so no one will find them. Zenny said that there have been some thieves from other tribes stealing their dragons' eggs. She asked me if she could send her egg here until it was ready to hatch so that it wouldn't be stolen. Zenny needed my help and so I said sure." Bella continued looking sheepishly down at the carpet, "Now that I think about it, I probably should have asked you first. Sorry Mom, but Zenny really needed my help."

"I don't want to cause you any trouble," groaned Skye, "I just want to save Zenny's egg from being stolen." A tear rolled down Skye's cheek.

"If I am understanding the two of you correctly, Skye, you came through a magic passageway from Krystal with a dragon egg to keep it from being stolen by another tribe?" asked Mom incredulously.

"Not just any egg Mom, Zenny and Warrior's first egg. It's golden which makes it ultra rare. Chief Tyee said there hasn't been one in like over 100 years," exclaimed Bella. "Mom, Zenny saved my life when I was in Krystal; the least I can do is to try to pay back her kindness and protect her precious baby."

"There really hasn't been a golden dragon egg in Krystal for over a century, and I would give up my own life to keep the egg safe. I would do absolutely anything, my people are depending on me," emphasized Skye.

"Okay, everyone settle down. So, girls, is there actually a dragon's egg in my house?" Mom inquired, raising her eyebrows, "a real dragon's egg right here in Canada?"

"Yes Mom," said Bella, "it's a really beautiful egg and it's Zenny's baby."

"First, I am very proud of you girls; you are both acting very bravely to help your friend. Second, I wish I would have known, then maybe we could have hatched a plan," said Mom laughing at her own joke.

"Oh Mom," groaned Bella, "you are too funny."

"Thank you, now I need to see this dragon's egg. Then the three of us are going to try to come up with a plan to protect this baby from the seismic scientist. Where did you hide the egg girls, is it under the bed?" laughed Mom.

"What is a scientist and why would they want the egg?" wailed Skye. "I thought I was coming here to be out of danger - not in even more danger."

Mom put her arm around Skye. "A scientist is someone who does research and discovers new things. Since dragons don't exist anywhere in our world, if he discovered one, he would be famous. That's not to mention the large amount of recognition he would get if he also discovered a girl from another world," explained Mom.

"You think he wants to capture me too, not just the egg?" Skye cried, "I just want to go home, this is much too scary."

"It will be okay. Skye, you are not afraid of dragons, and they are much bigger than a scientist so there's no need to fear. We will just need to come up with a plan to get you and the egg safely back to Krystal," declared Mom. "Now let me see this egg you have been hiding."

Bella smiled at Mom and got up and slowly opened her closet and reached for her laundry basket. She brought the basket over to Mom and set it down carefully, then she began to uncover the egg.

"Here is the beautiful egg," Bella announced. Mom and Skye both leaned over to see the egg. Mom let out a long breath with a look of amazement on her face.

"I can't believe what I'm seeing. Something that has always just been a myth is right here in front of me," confessed Mom.

"I agree with you Mom; when I fell into Krystal onto the back of a dragon, I thought I was dreaming. It took a few days for it to really sink in that Krystal and all of the amazing dragons were real. I was really scared at first, but Warrior's protective kindness helped a lot and then I met Zenny. I could communicate with her, and that helped me get over my fear," explained Bella.

"Even I had some fear when I started working in the keep. The dragons were so big and not all of them were as sweet as Zenny. It took some getting used to, I had to be brave until I gained confidence," remembered Skye.

The three of them just sat watching the egg for a while in utter amazement.

"Skye, how will we know when to send you home? Do you know when it is going to hatch?" enquired Mom. "If Zenny is anything like human parents, she definitely wants to be with her baby when it's born."

"Skye told me that she thought it would be two or three days until the egg started to flash and then we have two days to get home with the egg before the baby dragon hatches right here in Canada," explained Bella.

"Do you think we can stay safe for that long?" Skye asked hopefully. "This egg is really, really important to me and my tribe."

"Yes, we will keep you safe," assured Mom. "Let's start working on a plan."

Skye smiled a shaky smile and grabbed Mom's hand. Mom smiled back reassuringly. "I think this calls for some tea and cookies, lots of cookies, and a good brainstorming session. I will go pull the side blinds down and I will meet you both in the dining room in fifteen minutes. Remember to stay away from the windows in case that snoopy scientist is trying to spy on us."

Mom stood up to go and Bella rushed over to her and gave her a fierce hug.

"Thank you, Mom, you're the best, you always help us figure out just what to do," said Bella with tears in her eyes.

"We have been through a lot together honey bunny, we will get through this too," stated Mom as she left the bedroom. "Give me ten minutes before you come down so that the blinds are closed."

The girls both smiled at Mom as she left. Bella tucked the golden egg back into her laundry basket and put it carefully away in her closet and shut the door. Bella went and sat by Skye on the bed.

"I have decided to be brave, and not let this fear overtake me. I owe it to Zenny to have courage," declared Skye.

"I will be brave too. Zenny is worth whatever we have to do," agreed Bella.

Skye smiled at Bella and grabbed her hand. "We need to make a pledge. When we make a pledge in Krystal, we kind of put our forearms together and squeeze each others' elbows and then say the pledge together. Could we make a pledge to protect each other and the egg?" asked Skye hopefully.

"I think that's a great idea, then we will have more confidence in each other to do the right thing if we are ever faced with danger." The two girls stood up and clasped each other's right elbows. "I, Bella, solemnly pledge to protect Skye and to get Zenny's precious golden egg home no matter what danger we find ourselves in," pledged Bella.

"I, Skye, do pledge to be my bravest and to protect Bella, her Mom, and Zenny's egg no matter what dangers we find ourselves in," pledged Skye. The girls gave each other's arms an extra big squeeze and then headed downstairs to meet Mom.

The girls were extra careful to avoid the windows even though Mom had lowered the blinds. When they got to the dining room Mom was already there with a pad of paper and a pen. The girls smiled and sat on each side of Mom.

"I have been thinking of a couple of ideas. Which one of your friends does Skye look the most like?" asked Mom. They both looked at Skye and studied her face.

"I think she looks a lot like Page. What do you think?" asked Bella.

"I totally agree, that was exactly who I was thinking of," smiled Mom.

"How does who she looks like help us, Mom?" Bella wondered.

A big smile spread across Mom's face, "Let me explain."

Chapter 9

Tricking a Scientist

The two girls were getting ready for Skye's first night sleep in Canada after a productive brainstorming session with Mom. The girls had helped her carry the spare room's mattress into Bella's room and they placed it strategically in front of the closet so that Skye could guard the egg but still sleep peacefully.

"We have come up with a fantastic plan for us to fool that scientist, don't you think?" asked Skye.

"Yes, it seems pretty foolproof, but we will still have to be careful not to get too close to him or be seen by him for any long periods of time. Hopefully he won't know who is who when he sees us all together. Then we can pass you off as Page if we ever need to. We can't take any chances, he is a scientist after all, so he must be at least somewhat smart," laughed Bella.

The girls finished getting ready for bed and snuggled in under their covers.

"It was sure nice of your friend Page to be so willing to help with the plan, even though she doesn't know she is helping," laughed Skye.

"I think that's probably the safest for all of us, the fewer people who know the real story, the better. I wouldn't have believed it if I hadn't lived it. I could never have imagined there was another world out there," replied Bella.

"I can't believe that you and I are the only two people that have seen both worlds," confessed Skye, "that is pretty remarkable. It makes us really lucky I guess, but I was very scared when I went through that passageway," stated Skye.

"I believe you; I was really scared too when I had to come through the passage, but I really wanted to get back to my Mom. I really missed her, my home and my friends. It was funny though, when I got home, I missed Chief Tyee and Zenny a lot," Bella explained.

"I never thought of that," said Skye, "but you and your Mom are so kind. I'm sure I will miss you both too when I go back to Krystal. I am not missing Krystal that much right now because it was terrifying having enemies trying to steal the dragons' eggs and having to be on the lookout all the time." Skye turned on her side facing the closet and tucked the blanket under her chin, "Good night, Bella, thank you for everything that you have done for me and for my homeland of Krystal."

"You are welcome, Skye. I hope your first night's sleep here is a pleasant one. We will have some fun tomorrow at the mall. Good night, sleep tight," Bella said sleepily.

The house was quiet, Mom had gone to bed an hour ago and it didn't take Bella and Skye long to fall asleep after the very eventful day they had both had. It felt like only minutes had passed when dawn broke through Bella's window shortly after seven and it looked like it was going to be a beautiful sunny day. You could hear the Chickadees chirping happily in the maple tree in the backyard. Bella woke up smiling, pleased that there was a dragon's egg in her closet. Not just any dragon's egg, but Zenny's precious golden egg. She felt so honoured to be trusted by her friends to keep this egg safe. Bella had fallen asleep dreaming of her friends in Krystal and was still thinking about them now.

Skye began making a whimpering sound, Bella thought she must be having a dream. Then Skye called out 'NO, NO' and Bella knew she was having a nightmare.

"Skye, Skye," called Bella softly, "you are safe. You can wake up now. Everything is okay." Skye woke up with a start and bolted out of bed in a fighting stance both fists raised.

"You won't get the egg," she yelled. Skye was ready to swing at anything that moved.

"You are safe Skye; the egg is safe. If someone had tried to take it, they would have tripped right over you," chuckled Bella.

"Oh Bella, hi. I guess I was dreaming," said Skye with a small smile. She went over to the closet, moved the mattress and checked on the precious egg. It was snug and warm, wrapped in the blankets in the laundry basket just where they had left it the night before. Skye let out a sigh of relief.

"I think you were having a nightmare," said Bella.

"Do you mean a night terror?" Skye asked. "Yes, that's what it was. Did I hurt you?"

"No, you didn't hurt me, why do you ask?" Bella looked puzzled.

"Once or twice in the keep, when one of the trainers tried to wake me up, I kind of hit them. One of them even got a bloody nose. I felt really bad, and I got teased a lot about it from Chief Tyee and the trainers. They called me slugger Skye" laughed Skye. She sat back down on her mattress, looking embarrassed.

"That would have been good information to know before I woke you up," laughed Bella, "I'm really glad you didn't hit me." Light was peeking in the curtains and the girls were wide awake, so they got dressed and ready for breakfast and then went downstairs in search of mom and some delicious food.

"Good morning beautiful girls, I made pancakes for all of us for breakfast. I hope you like pancakes, Skye. They are one of Bella's favorite breakfast foods," said Mom.

"Any food with 'cake' in the name has to be good," laughed Skye, "Thank you for the morning meal. I really appreciate what you've done for me." Skye watched as Bella loaded her plate with pancakes and topped them with blue colored berries, thick syrupy stuff, and some white spray.

"Thanks Mom, this looks really delicious," said Bella hungrily. "Yummo!"

"What do I do?" asked Skye as she put three pancakes on her plate.

"You put on some blueberries and syrup and then spray on the whipped cream. I can help you with the spray cream if you like," said Mom.

"Yes please," said Skye, handing her plate to Mom. Mom took Skye's plate and added the blueberries and golden maple syrup and then tipped the whipped cream canister over and sprayed the whipped cream onto the pancakes in the shape of a happy face. Skye smiled at Mom as she took her plate back and went to sit beside Bella. Bella was half done with her first pancake. "The stories Chief Tyee told me about how much you like food were not exaggerated," laughed Skye.

"That's my Bella," chuckled Mom. "Famous in another world for the amount she can eat." Skye lifted her first bite of morning meal towards her mouth.

"This smells amazing," said Skye, as she slowly placed her first bite in her mouth. Bella and Mom watched closely as a smile spread across Skye's face, and she reached for her second bite.

"It tastes even better, right? Mmmmm," said Bella, stuffing another big bite into her mouth. When Mom was finally done cooking the pancakes, she sat down with the girls and loaded her plate. She had brought lots more pancakes with her for the girls to have seconds.

"These cakes are really good," said Skye, "what is that white stuff called again?"

"Whipped cream," said Bella, "we put it on other things too like pie, or sundaes."

"I think I would put this on everything. It's delicious, and it's enjoyable to spray," said Skye as she sprayed more whipped cream onto her plate, tipping the can over the way Mom had shown her. The three of them enjoyed eating a hearty breakfast together. Mom was pouring her second cup of coffee when there was a loud knock at the door.

"I will get the door; you two stay silent and don't leave the kitchen," Mom whispered as she got up to answer the door. "Who is it?" Mom called.

"It's Jason again from the University. Can I please talk to you and your daughter?" he asked. Mom opened the door to find Jason standing on the step holding a bunch of equipment. Mom started to chuckle at how ridiculous he looked.

"Good morning, Jason. Why are you here and what is all this equipment you have with you?" Mom asked suspiciously.

"Hello. I'm here in hopes of seeing your daughter. I would like to check her for radiation and subterranean particles. This equipment helps with my testing," indicated Jason pointing to his equipment.

"You will not be doing any sort of testing on my daughter, but I will allow you to speak to her," said Mom matter of factly. "Bella, please come to the doorway, but not a step further. Jason is back and would like a word with you." Bella came to the doorway of the living room.

"Hi, what do you want from me?" asked Bella, staring at Jason. Jason fidgeted with his clipboard while he got a pen from his pocket, almost dropping the large bunch of equipment that was over his shoulder. One large piece of metal equipment fell from his stack and landed firmly on his toe with a clatter. Mom began to laugh again.

"Ooooph," muttered Jason, "well, that will definitely leave a mark." He raised his gaze over to where Bella was standing and smiled. "Bella, I wanted to ask you if you have been feeling alright this week and if you've noticed any sudden growth spurts or weight changes?"

"Well Jason, I am feeling fine, thanks for asking, and I haven't grown in almost two years; as for my weight, that is seriously none of your business," stated Bella flatly.

"Yes yes, pardon me about the weight question," back peddled Jason, "what about sleeping and eating - any changes there?" Jason shifted side to side under the weight of the heavy equipment.

"No Jason, I eat a lot and sleep great," said Bella.

"Jason the interview is over, please leave now," said Mom firmly as she was closing the door.

"I still have lots of questions! What about bowel movements?" asked Jason hurriedly.

"Jason, that is certainly none of your business. We have humoured you a lot over these last two years, but this is the final straw. Leave us alone and stop watching our house or I will call the police and have you arrested. In case you are wondering, my front door security camera has recorded this whole bizarre conversation, so I have concrete proof that you have been harassing us. Leave now!" yelled Mom as she slammed the door. There was the sound of metal clattering on the sidewalk outside.

"I hope that landed on his other foot," said Mom, still angry at Jason for his intrusion and inappropriate questions.

"Way to go Mom, you sure told him. Thanks for defending me. What a snoopy jerk he is," said Bella. Bella hugged her Mom and they both went back into the kitchen to sit with Skye. Skye had a big smile on her face when they entered the room.

"You would make a great warrior," said Skye, grinning at Mom.

"Thank you," said Mom with a smile, "when my kid is threatened, I kind of turn into a momma bear." Mom brushed Bella's hair from her eyes with her fingertips. "Now I want you two girls to finish getting ready for the day so you can have some fun."

"Do you think it will be safe to take Skye shopping while that weird Jason is after us?" asked Bella worriedly.

"I think we should stick with our original plan with Page today and take you girls to the mall for some fun. Then after I get you dropped off, I will come right back here to guard the egg," said Mom determinedly.

Chapter 10

Stocking up on Crystals

The dawn brought the day to life beautifully in Krystal with a clear colorful sky filled with amazing purples, blues, and pinks decorating the horizon. It looked like a day for peace, not for preparing for an upcoming battle tomorrow. Alli was ready at daybreak with three lunches packed, one for her, Bade, and Chief Tyee. She also had some snacks for the dragons. Chief Tyee had already gone to the keep. He was getting Warrior and Zenny an early breakfast so that they could all set off before the sun was very far on its journey across the sky. Bade was getting his swords and arrows ready for his day of leading the tracking parties. "Here is a lunch for you, Bade. It is packed with love and warm cocoa," Alli said with a grin.

"Thank you, your lunches are always the best. I wish I was eating it with you though," sighed Bade.

"We both have important jobs to do today and once the battle is won tomorrow, we can have lunch together anytime," said Alli smiling.

"That sounds great, I will see you tonight," said Bade as he walked out of the front door headed in the direction of the clearing. When he had walked a few steps, he turned back to see Alli still watching him from the doorway. He smiled, waved, and then continued to walk toward the clearing; his heart filled with love for his caring betrothed...

Alli quickly finished getting ready to go, so they can gather the crystals that they might need for the battle. When she had everything she required, she walked out the front door towards the keep to meet Chief Tyee. It was only a short walk to the keep but he was already waiting for her with Warrior by his side.

"Are you finally ready?" asked Chief Tyee impatiently. Alli stuck out her tongue at her brother like she used to do as a child, and they both laughed together. Zenny came out of the door of the keep and the four of them set off toward the crystal cave. They walked in silence, enjoying the beautiful sunrise and warm weather. The terrain began getting steeper, the path narrower, and they had to continue their walk in single file. Warrior took the lead followed by Chief Tyee, Alli, and with Zenny bringing up the rear. They were almost to the cave of crystals enchanted entrance when Warrior suddenly stopped.

"What is it, boy?" asked Tyee quietly. Chief Tyee followed Warrior's gaze and then he saw it, another of the barbed arrows from the southernmost tribe. Warrior and Zenny instantly went on high alert, closing the distance between themselves and Alli to keep her safe. Chief Tyee got onto Warrior's back and reached up into the spruce tree to retrieve the arrow. "Look Alli, this arrow has even more murderous barbs than the last one. We need to stay on high alert. I'm going to scout ahead to make sure we can get to the cave of crystals safely. You stay here with Warrior and Zenny and try hard to stay silent."

"Okay, please stay safe my brother," whispered Alli. Chief Tyee set off towards the crystal cave and Alli stood between Warrior and Zenny watching Chief Tyee silently walk into the forest and then disappear. The group waited patiently until Chief Tyee reappeared as silently as he had left. Alli saw another broken arrow in his hand. "Welcome back brother, what have you discovered about our enemies?" inquired Alli.

"They had a camp about an hour's walk from here, the fire coals were cold so I'm not sure when the camp was last used, but they must have been hunting for food because I found some more broken arrows. I think we will be safe at the crystal cave, but we will have to watch going home in case they find our tracks and follow us," stated Chief Tyee worriedly.

"I'm very glad we have the dragons with us in case they start to attack us, and we have to take to the sky," said Alli.

"That would be a last resort for sure, I don't want them shooting our dragons with these awful arrows," said Chief Tyee in disgust. They finished their hike to the cave as silently as they could. Chief Tyee used his magic and opened the cave and removed the enchantment with an incantation. When the cave entrance was revealed, Chief Tyee and Alli entered the cave of crystals and the two brave dragons stood guard at the entrance. The cave was so full of crystals that they didn't even need a light to see. They both began searching for the magical green crystals they would need to use against their enemies to change them into mice. Chief Tyee was the first to find one. It was on the edge of a rock on the side of the cave. He dislodged the green crystal carefully and put it in his pouch. Alli found a group of red healing crystals, she picked up four and put them in her shoulder bag. Healing crystals may be needed in the battle. Chief Tyee was struggling to find any more of the green crystals, so he ventured further back; he had never been this far into the cave before. The passage became very narrow, but he thought he saw a glow from green crystals just up ahead. He got down on his hands and knees and began to crawl forward. He had only gone a short way when the passage took a sharp turn to the left and then almost immediately a sharp turn back to the right; the passage was so narrow now that he had to crawl along on his belly. Suddenly the tiny passage opened up to reveal a huge cavern filled with crystals of every shape, color, and size. There were even more colors than in the outer room. The chief couldn't believe his eyes or his luck. He wandered around the cavern first gathering green crystals and then choosing small samples of some of the other colors he had never seen before to show Alli. They could research them in the old scrolls and find out their uses. He crawled back into the tunnel and made his way as quickly as he could back to Alli.

"You are not going to believe what I found", said Chief Tyee excitedly.

"I hope it is more green crystals because I have only found one so far," answered Alli.

"Yes, I found more green crystals and an enormous room full of crystals of every color, even more colors than are in this room. I couldn't believe my eyes. I brought a few samples of the new colors. Maybe, when this is over, you will help me research them?" Chief Tyee asked hopefully.

Alli laughed, "You mean will I read through the old dusty scrolls until I find the information and then tell you about it?"

"Yes, something like that," said Chief Tyee with a boyish grin. They both laughed and packed up their bags with a few more crystals they might need as they walked towards the entrance and their awaiting dragons. The sun was bright when they exited the cave, causing them to squint. Zenny and Warrior were waiting patiently on guard for their return.

"Any signs of our enemies?" asked Chief Tyee. Warrior communicated to him that it had been quiet, but he had thought he caught a whiff of human when the breeze had picked up a short time ago although he can't smell it now. "Warrior thought he smelled a human a while ago but not now, so we will have to be extra vigilant on the way home," stated Chief Tyee to Alli. Alli could not communicate with Warrior.

Warrior set out first along the path, leaving a huge dark shadow for the rest to walk in. Chief Tyee and Alli followed with Zenny bringing up the rear and protecting their backs. They walked towards home for a couple of hours and then stopped to have their lunch and give the dragons the snacks Alli had brought for them. They were just finishing up their lunch and having a drink of water when Warrior communicated that he smelled human again and that it was getting stronger. Chief Tyee signaled to Alli to move off of the path and into the trees behind a large outcropping of rocks that was just a few metres off the trail, thankfully it was big enough for the dragons to hide behind as well. When everyone was safely hidden Chief Tyee walked stealthily down through the trees to see if he could find the source of the smell. He walked about 20 metres when he heard a voice coming towards him, he stopped and quickly hid behind a nearby tree and waited. About ten minutes later a single man with a large bow and quiver of arrows came into view. He was carrying a few small squirrels he had killed. The man was talking to himself and complaining about the other men in his hunting party. The outsider had no idea that he was being watched by Chief Tyee. The Chief watched and listened carefully to determine if the man was truly alone and not just ahead of the rest of the invaders.

Chief Tyee quickly devised a plan to overpower and capture this enemy. He got an orange crystal out of his pouch and felt it begin to warm in his hands and waited until his boots became invisible and then silently, he started after the enemy. The man was very large and had a very strong smell. 'No wonder Warrior could smell him from miles away,' thought Chief Tyee. He moved quickly and silently to get ahead of his enemy and then he lunged at him, making direct contact. The man hit the ground with a hard ooof. Chief Tyee quickly grabbed the rope that was attached to his enemies' squirrel catch and began to tie his enemy's hands.

"Don't make a sound and I won't hurt you!" said Chief Tyee menacingly as he finished tying his enemies' hands securely. The man was in such shock that when Chief Tyee began to reappear, the man started to shake with fear. He was a big man, at least a head taller than Chief Tyee and at least a stone heavier. He was dressed in poorly sewn furs and was carrying two large sacks, one over each of his shoulders. Chief Tyee was glad he had had the element of surprise because this man could have put up a good fight.

"What are you?" the man asked in a whisper. Chief Tyee did not answer but instead helped the man up off the ground onto his feet. Chief Tyee began leading the man toward the location where Alli and the dragons were hiding. When he got closer to the hiding place, he could hear Warrior begin to snort; he was bravely trying to warn Alli that the enemy was close by. Alli was unable to understand Warrior because she had not been able to connect to him.

"It's okay Warrior, I have captured our enemy and am bringing him towards you," said Chief Tyee. Warrior gave another snort but then was quiet. Chief Tyee brought the large man into view and Alli gasped.

Warrior snorted loudly. The prisoner's eyes grew wide, and he began to shake at the sight of the massive dragons.

"What are we going to do with that?" asked Alli, holding her nose and looking at the oversized smelly man.

"I am not sure yet, but I'd like to get him secured in the 'dungeon' with a strong guard until we decide what to do with him," said Chief Tyee. Alli gave Chief Tyee a questioning look. She knew they didn't have a dungeon.

"Maybe the guards could hose him and his clothes down. He smells so bad it hurts my nose," said Alli wrinkling up her nose. The prisoner just hung his head and remained quiet. The group began the walk towards home and the armories. When they came to the fork in the road leading to the armories Chief Tyee stopped. "We haven't seen any more signs of his friends, so I think it's safe to take him to the dungeon on my own," said Chief Tyee confidently.

"Are you sure about that?" questioned Alli.

"Alli, I don't want this ruffian to know where our home is, although I suspect he already might know where it is and unfortunately maybe he knows a whole lot more about us," said Chief Tyee giving the prisoner a scornful glance. "I'm going to take him to the dungeon with Warrior right now. You and Zenny go home. When you see Bade please ask him to come and give me his report and to bring some guards to the dungeon to take charge of our captive."

"Stay safe my brother, we will go as quickly as we can, if he gives you any trouble just let Warrior eat him," Alli said angrily. The prisoner had a look of horror on his face at Alli's words as he looked up at the big black dragon. Alli and Zenny took off at a very fast pace toward home to get Bade's help for Chief Tyee at the armouries. Chief Tyee set off leading the prisoner on foot. Warrior was on alert and sniffing deeply to detect the presence of any more humans. It was hard for Chief Tyee to smell anything but the very stinky man beside him, but he was very vigilant with his senses of hearing and sight, constantly scanning the horizon for any signs of movement. When they arrived at the armouries Chief Tyee decided to put on a big show of magic for his superstitious friend. When he began taking off the enchantment to open the hill in front of the armouries, he performed a great chanting and dancing routine to the spirit of the mountain and when the armouries began to open, the prisoner fell to his knees in fear. Chief Tyee smiled, 'mission accomplished' he thought to himself as he unlocked the huge metal door. He helped the shaking man up and led him into the front hall with all its very large intimidating metal doors and the man was so shocked he froze just inside the entryway. Chief Tyee decided to just leave him there and went back to the door to communicate with Warrior. "Hello friend. Would you like to squeeze into the 'dungeon' like when you were young," Chief Tyee asked Warrior with a smile, "or hide outside and watch for any more enemies?"

"I will hide behind the outcropping of rock just above the entrance to the 'dungeon', the doorway scrapes my wings now that I am so large, and I want them to be in prime shape for tomorrow's battle. The evergreen trees arc thick there and will provide me with a good cover just like when we used to play 'hide and go seek' as kids." communicated Warrior.

Chief Tyee smiled at the happy memory Warrior had shared. "That is a great hiding spot for you, I will leave the entrance door open and if I need you to eat him, I will just call you," said Chief Tyee with a smile. Warrior gave a loud snort and started up towards his hiding spot and Chief Tyee went back inside to guard the smelly prisoner and wait for Bade.

Alli and Zenny had made it home in record time. When they got close to the keep, they could see Bade approaching and Alli began to wave excitedly and call out. When Bade saw them without Chief Tyee and Warrior he knew something was wrong and he began to run towards them as fast as his tired legs could go. "Alli, what's happened, are you okay, is anyone hurt? Where's Tyee?" shouted Bade frantically.

Alli ran toward Bade and flew into his arms as she explained, "Tyee caught a large, very smelly enemy, and took him to the armouries which he called 'the dungeon'. He needs you to bring guards as quickly as you can to help him."

"I'm so glad that no one was hurt. How did you manage to capture a big smelly man?" asked Bade with a chuckle. Zenny left the pair to discuss the prisoner and she went into the keep to eat some food and get a much-needed drink of water. She also needed to start preparing the other dragons for tomorrow's battle.

"I don't know how he captured the smelly man, the dragons and I were hiding behind some big rocks and trees to stay safe because Warrior had smelled a human and Tyee was just supposed to be scouting ahead. The next thing we knew, he was back with the big smelly prisoner," exclaimed Alli.

Bade began to smile, then to laugh, "That sounds like our Chief, always full of surprises. I will round up some men from the village to help guard the prisoner. We had a very successful scouting expedition. We found their camp and we even saw one of the dragon eggs that was stolen, hopefully the other one is there too," said Bade happily. Alli ran back into his arms and gave him another hug.

"That's the best news, you did have a truly successful day. I truly hope the other egg is there too. It would be so great to be able to get both eggs back to their mothers. I will quickly make some food for you to take up to the 'dungeon' while you organize some brave villagers to aid the Chief," chuckled Alli.

"I really hope that food includes some warm cocoa for yours truly," smiled Bade.

"Of course, it will, you deserve a special treat after your busy and productive day. I'm really proud of you, Bade," said Alli lovingly. Bade hurried away to find guards as Alli went into the house to get food and water ready for Bade to take to Warrior and her brother Chief Tyee. Alli wished her brother wouldn't take so many chances, but he was a very brave leader for their people and always put the well being of the tribe before his own.

Within half an hour Bade was back, knocking on Alli's door with four big burly volunteers to help guard the prisoner. Alli had a large basket of food for everyone and another basket of water bottles and dragon snacks for Warrior.

"Thank you Alli," said Bade, smiling. Alli returned the smile warmly.

"Don't worry, there is warm cocoa in the food basket for you," Alli said with a chuckle. Bade gave Alli a small kiss on the cheek, and the men grinned. Bade blushed, as the group set off quickly with the baskets to help their Chief. Alli watched them go and then went back into the house to practice with the crystals so she would be prepared for tomorrow's battle.

The men walked quickly and quietly with their senses on heightened alert for any sign of their enemy. It wasn't a long walk compared to the distance the men had traveled in search of the enemy's camp, but they were tired and on edge about the impending battle tomorrow and it made the distance seem endless. All of these men had families that they cared about and needed to protect so the thought of battle tomorrow was weighing heavily on their minds. When they arrived at the 'dungeon' they found the door open and Chief Tyee standing on guard just inside the armouries. He was in front of a big man who was sitting silently on the floor. The smelly man looked like he was praying.

"Hello friends, it's so nice to see you," said Chief Tyee, "I am pleased to have reinforcements. Warrior, come down please, I see some dragon snacks and some water Alli has sent for you," called Chief Tyee. The men were surprised when the dragon appeared, no one had seen him or even suspected he was watching from above the armories. Bade got out the dragon snacks and poured some water for Warrior. Warrior drank all his water quickly and then started on his snacks enjoying every bite of the delicious fruits. "Looks like you were thirsty Warrior, I'm glad that Alli sent you some sustenance," said Chief Tyee, patting Warrior's neck.

"Men, this is the prisoner you must guard. Don't take him down to the deep 'dungeon' because we will take him with us tomorrow into the battle and use him as a bargaining chip instead of placing him in the chains. Do not let him escape, if he tries you must stop him at any cost."

The men smirked at Chief Tyee's words because they knew that Krystal didn't have a deep dungeon or chains to use on anyone. They also knew their duty and how important it was to guard their captive.

The men posted two guards inside the armouries and two at the entrance.

Bade tried to give Chief Tyee some of the food but he refused. "Leave the food for the men, I will eat when I get home," said Chief Tyee respectfully. Bade and Chief Tyee set off toward home with Warrior close behind them. "Bade, what is your report from today?" inquired Chief Tyee. "I have good news. We found their camp and we saw one of the missing eggs still unhatched, there was no sign of the other egg though," said Bade.

"Oh, that is welcome news, I'm pleased we will be able to recover at least one of the eggs as well as get rid of these intruders once and for all," said Chief Tyee with a relieved sigh. "Where did you finally find their camp, and how big is their raiding party?"

"Their present camp is on the far west side of our land past the main village. They only have about 30 people in the camp and that includes both male and female warriors. We were surprised when we even spotted a couple of children in their camp," said Bade.

"Children? Who would bring children on a raid?" asked Chief Tyee disgustedly. "These people really are ruthless. We will have to be careful when we launch our attack tomorrow not to hurt the children. There are also a lot of sheep on that side of the village; we will have to watch for those too."

"I could tell the villagers to bring the sheep into the close pens tonight so they will be safe and out of the way for tomorrow's battle," suggested Bade.

"That's a great idea but warn them not to go too far west looking for sheep, we don't want anyone getting captured," said Chief Tyee.

The two walked quickly toward Chief Tyee's house with Warrior right behind them guarding their every step. When they arrived back at Chief Tyee's house, Bade went to warn the villagers to bring in the livestock, and Chief Tyee went to the keep to feed and water Warrior and make sure the strong dragons were all ready for tomorrow.

Chapter 11

Going to the Mall

The girls were so excited that Mom thought it was still safe to go to the mall they let out small squeals and hurried excitedly up the stairs to shower and get ready for their exciting day. Mom busied herself cleaning up the breakfast dishes. An hour later the girls came downstairs smiling and looking like happy, carefree teenagers. Skye had her hair in a ponytail through the back of a ball cap and was carrying sunglasses. Bella also had a ball cap on with a ponytail pulled through. They were both wearing Bella's clothes, jeans and blue t-shirts. Mom was surprised at how much Skye looked like Page.

"My, don't you two clean up well! Skye, you look great in Bella's clothes," chuckled Mom. "That was a great idea wearing the ball caps that will help to hide your pretty faces from Jason." Mom smiled admiringly at the eager girls. "Are you excited to see the mall, Skye?"

"I am so excited and a bit nervous. Riding in the car was both fun and a little scary all at the same time. I've never seen a mall, so I'm really excited to learn what a mall is, but I'm also a little nervous" said Skye happily. The girls made themselves comfortable at the kitchen counter and watched Mom finish wiping the table.

"I need to leave in ten minutes to pick up Page," said Bella, "then you two leave 'incognito' after that to meet us at the mall," said Bella using air quotes and making Mom laugh.

"You girls will have fun today," said Mom, as she reached for her purse. "I want to give you each $50.00 so that you can buy a special lunch and Skye, maybe you could get a keepsake to take home with you to Krystal?" Mom handed each girl a bright red $50.00 dollar bill.

"This is very pretty, thank you," said Skye as she took the red paper from Mom. Bella and Mom both smiled.

"Yes, thanks a lot Mom, I really appreciate this money. It does actually look pretty, but this is what you use to get something you really like, maybe a shirt or a purse. Is there anything at home that you wish you had or something that you need?" Bella asked.

"Oh, I understand now. You use this to trade for other things." Mom and Bella nodded. "There is something I wish I had for winter, some woollen socks. The wolves have been getting some of the sheep this year and there's not enough wool to go around so I keep fixing and mending my three precious pairs of woollen socks. I would love a pair without holes or maybe some different colored mending wool for a change. Do they have socks at your mall?" asked Skye curiously.

"They definitely have socks at the mall, they have so many socks that it might even be hard for you to choose," said Mom with a smile.

"It's time for me to go now," said Bella as she grabbed her purse and got out her car keys. "I will pick up Page and then meet you at the mall by the bus entrance so it will look like Skye just got off the bus if 'JA-son' is following you." Bella scrunched up her face like saying the name Jason smelled bad and everyone laughed.

"I will have your water bottle to give to you so that it looks like you just forgot it and I'm dropping it off. I will park in the unloading zone and slide out the passenger side right after Skye sneaks into a bus crowd. Skye will keep a close eye on me to see where to meet you and Page. Then it's right back home for me to guard this precious baby egg. Does everyone understand and agree with our plan?" questioned Mom. Both girls nodded their heads in affirmation.

"I've got it," said Bella, "just remember to wait for a crowd before you start to get out, and Page and I will be there to meet you, no problem."

"Could you keep this safe for me, please? I don't have anything to carry it in," Skye asked as she handed her money to Bella.

"Sure, no problem," said Bella as she tucked the money into her purse. They walked Bella to the front door, Skye stayed hidden inside and Mom went out to watch in case Jason, the scientist, was still there waiting to follow Bella. Bella got in and started up her little red car. Mom waved while she waited and watched carefully for any signs of Jason but after five minutes of not seeing anything suspicious, she went back inside.

"Any signs of him?" asked Skye worriedly.

"No," Mom said, shaking her head, "I must have put the fear of Mom into him."

Skye laughed; "I am glad you are on my side."

Mom grabbed her purse and keys and headed toward the front garage followed closely by Skye carrying the water bottle. Mom opened the front passenger door and pulled the blanket off of the seat and spread it across the floor. She put the front seat as far back as it would go to give Skye more room.

"Okay Skye, you get in and make yourself comfortable on the floor, while I walk around to make sure you can't be seen from anywhere outside the car." Skye proceeded to get into the car and curl into a tiny ball on the floor as Mom shut the car door. Mom discovered that from the driver's side Skye might be seen by cars passing her so she ran upstairs and got another blanket to throw over Skye so there would be no chance of discovery.

"Okay just put this blanket over you and there will be no chance of you being seen from any angle," said Mom confidently.

"You think of everything, thank you," said Skye as she covered herself with the blanket. Mom pushed the garage door opener and waited for the big door to rise to the top. She turned the key in the ignition and the car came to life. Mom slowly backed out of the garage and onto the street, closing the garage door with the remote as she went.

"That button opened and closed the big door," observed Skye. "Bella said you didn't have magic in Canada. That seems like magic to me."

"I guess it is pretty handy to be able to open a door with the push of a button," said Mom. Mom put on the brakes and stopped the car at a streetlight.

"Are we there already?" asked Skye. "I'm a little scared."

"It won't be long until we are there but right now, we are just at a red stoplight. We have lights that tell the drivers of the cars when to stop and when to go. They make driving safer for everyone, even the people who are walking," Mom explained.

"The only way I get around is my two feet and a heartbeat," laughed Skye, "plus the occasional wonderful dragon ride."

"When I was your age that's how I got around too, minus the dragon rides of course," laughed Mom. The car was moving again, Skye was riding quietly on the floor of the car. Mom turned on the signal light and Skye could feel the car begin to slow down again. "We are just turning into the parking lot," said Mom, "are you ready to have fun and see a Canadian mall?"

"I'm as ready as I will ever be," said Skye, taking a deep breath.

Mom stopped the car in the drop off area beside the bus zone and sent a text to Bella. Her phone quickly buzzed as Bella answered back. "Okay, Bella and Page are walking this way and will be here in about a minute," Mom said as she got Bella's water bottle ready to go. There's a big bus just starting to unload; when I move the blanket, make sure your hat is down and your glasses are on. When I open the door, get out and wait until some people from the bus are behind you. Then you can stand up and walk in with them. Keep watching me, I will get ahead of you and then you will see where Bella and Page are. She will be watching for you and pretend to run into you like an old friend. Got it?"

"I understand and will do my best to blend in," declared Skye while she straightened her hat and put on her sunglasses. Mom slid over and opened the passenger door just as a large group of people got off the bus. Skye slid out the door and stayed low until she had made it into the crowd and then she stood up and blended in. Mom hurried and got in front of her and went through the doors with the crowd. She saw Bella and Page waiting for her by the Coffee House, and she waved. The girls waved back, and Mom gave Bella her water bottle. They visited for a minute while Mom grabbed a quick coffee. Mom hugged Bella goodbye and walked back to her car, constantly on the lookout for Jason.

Chapter 12

Shopping

Bella saw Skye enter the mall and she had kept an eye on her progress. Skye was looking in the shop windows with awe, she could not believe how many beautiful things she saw and how many people there were in one place. She was admiring a beautiful jewel bracelet in a shop window when she heard her name being called and she turned to see Bella and her friend Page. Page was also wearing a ball cap, jeans, and a light blue t-shirt.

"Skye, is that you?" Bella asked with a smile, "I haven't seen you in a while. How have you been?"

"Hi Bella, it's so nice to see you," answered Skye, "it's been too long. I'm fine. How are you?"

"I'm doing well, Skye, this is my friend Page. Hey Page, If it's okay with you, could Skye tag along with us?" asked Bella.

"It's nice to meet you Skye, of course you are welcome to shop with us. The more, the merrier, and I love your style. Blue is my favorite color," said Page cheerfully.

"It's nice to meet you too Page, I would love your shopping company," Skye smiled. The girls set off together down the mall looking in all the shops.

Mom had made it home and safely into the garage. She thought there had been a blue car following her, but then it turned a street ahead of her. Mom went directly upstairs to check on the egg. Everything was just where it had been, but Mom moved the mattress and opened the closet door to check anyway. She sat down on the edge of the bed and stared in awe at the beautiful egg.

"You are definitely an amazing little baby; I can't believe dragons are real," Mom said as she gently touched the egg. She could feel small vibrations and what felt like a heartbeat. She watched the egg for a long time and then covered it back up, closed the closet and put the mattress back in place. "See you in a couple of hours, precious baby dragon."

Mom busied herself cleaning up a little. Since their old bulldog had died the house was sure less messy but a lot quieter and lonelier when Bella wasn't home. It was a beautiful day, so Mom decided to do a bit of gardening before she checked on the dragon baby again.

The girls were having a great time at the mall. Skye was trying hard to act like everyone else and was fitting in convincingly. Bella was always on the lookout for Jason but hadn't seen even a hint of him so far. "I'm getting hungry," said Page, "how about the food court for lunch?"

"That sounds great," said Bella, "I would love some Pizza."

"Yes, that sounds really good to me," agreed Skye, smiling. The girls walked towards the center of the mall. The delicious smells were getting stronger the closer they got to the large food court. Skye looked around at all the different people lined up to eat so many different kinds of food.

"I think I'm going to get Souvlaki and Greek Salad," said Page. "I will meet you over at the Pizza Palace, keep your eyes open for a table." Page walked toward the Greek food restaurant and Bella took Skye towards the Pizza Palace.

"You are going to love pizza," said Bella as they lined up in the pizza queue.

"I love the smell already and it's fun to say Pizza. Pizza, pizza, pizzzzah," said Skye with a giggle. Bella ordered two slices of double cheese and two slices of Hawaiian pizza, as well as two root beer floats for them to drink. Bella also sneakily gave Skye her $50.00 from Mom to put in her pocket to buy some socks later. The girls picked up the trays of food and turned to find Page. Page had already skillfully found an empty table and was waving them over.

"Thanks Bella, this is overwhelming and exciting all at the same time," whispered Skye. "I can't wait to eat this delicious pizzzzah," laughed Skye again. The girls started walking toward Page to join her at the table for four. Page was wiping the table with some disposable hand wipes she had in her purse.

"This table was clean, but an extra wipe is always a good idea," said Page as the girls joined her. Page passed out hand wipes to the girls.

"Thanks Page, hygiene is always important. I should get some wipes for my purse too," said Bella.

"Thank you, Page, I like to wash my hands before meals," chimed in Skye. Page started eating her Greek salad first and Skye was watching Bella, so she could learn how to eat her pizza. First, Bella unwrapped her straw and put it into her root beer float, and then she picked up her pizza by the crust and took a bite. Skye copied Bella's example and lifted her first slice towards her, and it smelled delicious. She closed her eyes and took her first bite, a smile spreading across her face.

"This is scrumptious," said Skye, taking her second bite.

"Of course it is, it's carbs," said Page, poking at her salad. "I have to try really hard to stay away from them because the gluten makes me sick."

"I'm sorry Page, I should have gotten something else," said Bella as she set down her pizza back on her box.

"No, I'm glad you got pizza, at least I can smell it and imagine eating it. My Mom does make me gluten free pizza at home, with all my favourite toppings of course, so I am pretty lucky that I can eat pizza once in a while."

"Your Mom is really great," said Bella. Skye smiled, nodded her agreement, and kept happily eating her pizza.

"Yes, she is," smiled Page, "I think I will get her a couple of her favourite peppermint hot chocolate bombs on the way out from the chocolate shop to remind her how great she is."

"Those sound really good, I haven't had them from the chocolate shop," said Bella. The girls finished eating their meals and were just finishing their drinks when Page got a text.

"Speaking of Mom, she will be here in an hour to pick me up, I asked her to meet me over by the chocolate shop entrance. I hope that's okay?" asked Page.

"That's great, I really want to see what a chocolate bomb looks like," said Skye. The girls finished their lunches and Skye slurped the bottom of her root beer float. She looked up at the girls sheepishly. "Ooops, sorry," she said. The girls laughed as they went to empty their trays into the trash. They began to walk towards the chocolate shop. On the way there, there was a really cute light blue hoodie in the teen shop window. Page looked at it admiringly.

"What a fantastic hoodie, I think I should try to save up for it. If I do some extra chores at home and for my grandma, I will be able to earn it in no time," said Page.

"It would look great on you, it's the perfect color," said Bella.

"It will make you look even more beautiful, and it will bring out your eyes." said Skye, smiling at Page.

"Thanks guys," Page blushed. They kept going and passed a pet store. Skye stopped and looked at the small animals.

"We can come back here and look at the animals, if you like Skye, after we get Page to the chocolate shop," Instructed Bella.

"I would like that very much," Skye replied, as she hurried after the girls. When Bella opened the door for Page, Skye couldn't believe how good the chocolate smelled.

"This shop smells so good," said Skye, inhaling deeply. There was an employee giving samples of milk chocolates and he offered one to each of the girls.

"I'm glad you like our shop," said the kind employee whose name tag said Tanner, "please help yourselves to a sample of our creamy milk chocolate."

"Hi Tanner," laughed Page, "I haven't seen you in what, maybe a week?"

"Hi Page. It is always great to see one of our best customers, and you brought friends. I hope you all enjoy the samples of our smooth gluten free milk chocolate." Tanner winked at Page.

"Thanks Tanner, don't mind if I do! Thanks for reassuring me that it's gluten free. I really appreciate you and this shop." Page beamed, "I am going to get some hot chocolate bombs for my Mom. I hope you have some peppermint ones left."

Tanner went behind the counter and showed Page where the hot chocolate bombs were while the girls enjoyed eating their chocolate samples.

"Looks like you are in luck, Page. There are two peppermint, two dark chocolate, and two orange cream ones left," said Tanner as he checked the display case.

"Can I please get the two peppermint bombs for my Mom?" asked Page. "She's picking me up any minute and she loves your hot chocolate bombs." Tanner smiled and boxed up the two bombs and put in a couple of extra pieces of milk chocolate samples for Page. "Thanks Tanner, you are so good to me," grinned Page as she paid for her purchase.

"You are welcome," smiled Tanner, "Now, is there anything I can get for your friends?" he asked.

"I will take your other four hot chocolate bombs please, said Bella with a grin, they look lonely." Tanner laughed and boxed up the four remaining hot chocolate bombs. Bella paid Tanner and then left the store to meet Page's Mom. They got to the exit doors and Page looked out, her` Mom was just pulling up and Page and Bella waved. Page's Mom waved back and pulled up into the loading zone.

"Thanks for the great day, I had a lot of fun. It was also nice meeting you, Skye. Maybe we could get together again sometime," said Page as she opened the car door and slid into the front seat.

"It was very nice to meet you. I had a great day too! Thanks for letting me tag along," said Skye.

"Thanks for shopping today, Page. We will definitely have to do it again soon," Bella said with a smile. Page closed the car door and with one last wave her Mom drove away.

Bella saw a movement out of the corner of her eye but looked again and didn't see anyone. The girls went back into the mall and into the pet store. Bella told Skye about the different types of fish and birds that were in the store. Skye was surprised how many kinds of animals you could see in just one place.

"There are more different kinds of animals here than in all of Krystal," Skye said in amazement. "We catch fish for food, but they aren't small and pretty like these." They kept walking and Bella took Skye to the cat room. Skye was scared at first but soon found a small orange cat that she was brave enough to pet.

"If you like kittens, just wait until you see the puppies. They are my favourite," exclaimed Bella. The girls left the cat room and headed towards the puppy area. There were wire circular pens with different colors and sizes of fur-babies. Bella knelt down at the first pen and began to pet the light brown puppy that ran up to her. He was so cute with his curly hair and tiny bark. Skye went to the next pen where there was a larger brown and white bundle of fur. She knelt down and the big bundle came bounding up to her and she gathered her courage and put her hand through the bars and began to pet the big furball. A smile spread across her face. When another younger girl came and knelt by the pen, Skye got up and went to another pen with four very small bundles of fluff running around, she knelt down and put both hands through the bars to pet the excited puppies. Skye had never had a small pet before, the closest thing to a pet she'd had would be a dragon and they were so much bigger and more independent than these sweet little pups. Skye was sure she would love to have one of these little pets to love and care for.

"Which one is your favorite?" Bella asked Skye as she knelt beside her.

"I really love these small white ones; I wish we had these in

Krystal. It would be so nice to have one to care for. Which one is your favourite?" Skye asked Bella.

"I really like the little tan colored poodle that I was petting, he's so friendly and cute. I've come to visit him before a couple of times, he's been here a while and no one has taken him home, but I really think he's the best one. I would love a new dog to care for… our dog died a long time ago," said Bella longingly. We better get going to the wool shop so you can purchase your socks and then it will be time to go home." Skye gave the puppies one more pet and then got up to follow Bella.

"It's hard to leave them there, they are so cute," Skye glanced back at the pet store. "I'm sorry your dog died, what was it like having a dog to care for?" asked Skye.

"Until I met dragons, I thought my bulldog was pretty big," laughed Bella. "It was a lot of fun to have a dog; whenever you came into the house, she was always super excited to see you. She didn't have much of a tail so she would just wag her whole bum, it was really cute," remembered Bella. The girls were almost at the wool shop and Skye was getting even more excited.

"I can't believe you have a whole store for wool; at home I just go to my neighbors," stated Skye.

"We have a store for almost anything you could think of," said Bella. The girls arrived at the wool store that had colorful fluffy pictures of sheep in the window.

"Our sheep do not look like that," laughed Skye, "but if they did, I would pick the pink one's wool to make my socks." Bella laughed as the girls made their way farther into the store and towards the side wall covered in colorful socks. "Ooooh, there are so many beautiful colors," exclaimed Skye excitedly. Bella helped her choose two special pairs and then they went to look at the wool that was on clearance. Skye could afford two balls of purple wool along with her socks. When they got to the checkout, the older clerk smiled at them.

"Hello there young ladies, It's so nice to see young people who like to craft," said the clerk as she began ringing in Skye's purchases.

"I love to make my own socks; I have even made a few pairs for friends and family." Skye said excitedly. "I have never seen so many beautiful colors as you have here in your store." The clerk smiled at Skye's enthusiasm.

"I might just have a special deal for you if you are interested. A good customer of mine had ordered an Afghan kit and the company I ordered it from sent a baby blanket kit by mistake." The clerk bent down and got a large plastic bag out from under the counter and smiled as she watched Skye's eyes light up. "The company is replacing the kit free of charge so I have this baby blanket kit I don't need. I would like to give to you, if you like pink, that is?" said the clerk.

Skye nodded her acceptance excitedly, "Thank you! That is very kind, I love pink, it's my favorite color in the sunrise." said Skye enthusiastically. The clerk put the kit into Skye's bag and the girls left the store. "Thank you again," said Skye, waving. The clerk waved back. Bella thought she saw Jason just down the hallway and quickly turned Skye toward the exit.

"I think Jason might be here, I guess we didn't completely fool him with my friend from school, let's hurry to my car," gasped Bella. The two girls began walking quickly towards the exit. They got to the exit just as a bus was unloading and they blended in quickly with the passengers and then ran to Bella's car. They made it safely and hopped in, quickly locking the doors. Bella texted Mom that they thought they had seen Jason. Mom texted back that she would be outside waiting for them and would get them safely into the house. The girls buckled up and Bella started her little car. Bella drove her car as fast as she could towards home, frequently checking for signs of Jason's car behind them. They arrived home a few minutes later and Mom was waiting in the driveway holding her cell phone and a broom. The girls got out of the car and Mom motioned for them to go into the house. Mom started walking with her broom towards the blue car that had turned the corner to their house. Mom waved the broom menacingly at the car, and it quickly turned and sped away. Mom went back to join the girls in the house.

"You really are a brave warrior," said Skye as she gave Mom a hug. Mom hugged Skye back.

"Thanks Skye, I would do anything to keep you two safe," admitted Mom, "even if it means threatening Jason with my broom." The girls laughed and Bella gave her Mom a huge hug as well.

"Thanks for being so awesome Mom, I love you bunches and buckets," said Bella.

"I love you too sweetheart, forever and always," said Mom smiling at Bella.

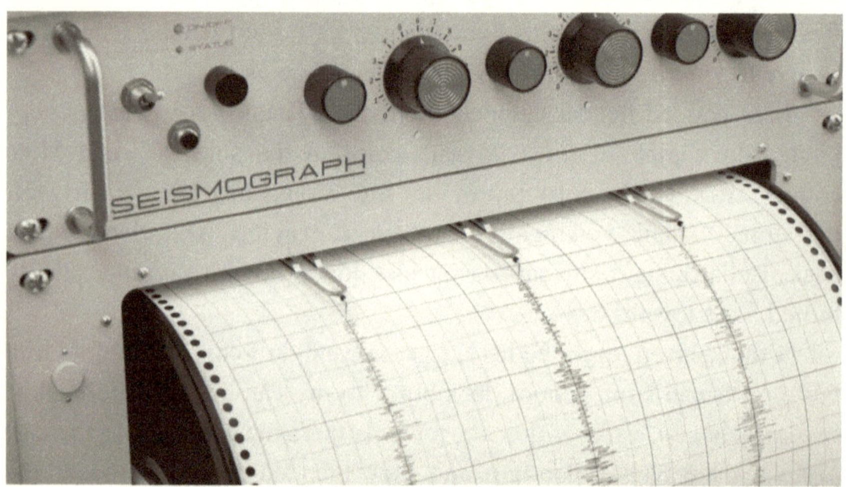

Chapter 13

Changes

"Now I have something exciting to show you." The girls followed Mom up to Bella's room and helped her move the mattress from in front of the closet. When they lifted the blanket, they could see a faint glow in the egg. "Wait for it," said Mom excitedly. Just then the egg began to flash three times with a lightning bolt pattern emanating from the egg. Skye inhaled sharply. Bella was holding her breath and staring at the egg.

"That's amazing," said Bella as she breathed out.

"I have seen a lot of dragon's hatch before, but I have never seen an egg like this!" Skye said in awe of the golden egg. "This dragon is definitely special; it is going to mean so much to our tribe."

"It flashed for the first time two hours ago. I got scared the first time it happened then watched in amazement as this little dragon let us know that they are going to enter this world very soon." Mom explained.

"I will have to contact Zenny tonight and arrange a time in the next two days to get the two of you safely back to her," announced Bella as she locked eyes with Skye.

"I am a little scared to go back through the passage," admitted Skye ashamedly, "I think sometimes I should be braver."

"Let me ask you something," said Mom, "Are you going to take this precious egg back through the tunnel?"

"Of course, I am," assured Skye.

"Well, that makes you very courageous because courage is when you are afraid to do something, but you are going to do it anyway. Both of you girls have shown that you are very brave and courageous with all you've already done to help your friends," stated mom matter of factly.

"Thank you," said both girls in unison. "That means a lot to me," Skye smiled at Mom.

"I am going to go and put the finishing touches on some supper for my two brave girls, and afterwards we can put our heads together and work out a plan to get you home. I also want to hear all about your day at the mall." Mom said as she left and headed towards the kitchen.

The girls sat silently watching the egg waiting for the flashing to begin again. They both jumped when the egg began to glow. They looked at each other and began to laugh simultaneously.

"We were both waiting for it to start flashing and it took us both by surprise anyways," laughed Bella. They watched the egg go through its cycle of glowing and flashing lightning bolts and then they tucked it back away under the soft blankets. Bella gently closed the closet doors and put the mattress back in front of them. "Let's go down for supper. It smells so delicious."

"That is a great idea. My stomach has been talking to me ever since that delicious smell wafted up here," agreed Skye. The girls walked downstairs and into the dining room. Mom had the table set for the three of them and she was just walking through the door carrying a large platter of her signature lasagna. Skye took a big breath in through her nose, "Whatever that amazing smell is, I'm looking forward to eating it." Skye licked her lips in anticipation.

"That smell is my mom's famous lasagna; it is one of my favorite foods. Thank you for making it Mom, what a great surprise," said Bella appreciatively. They all took their seats at the table and Mom poured everyone some ice water.

"I hope you are both hungry. I made an extra big batch, and I made us a nice salad to go along with it. I used vegetables from the garden to make the salad. Garden vegetables are always so fresh and good." Mom passed the salad bowl to Bella and began cutting the steaming lasagna. Bella took a big helping of salad and covered it in salad dressing. She passed the bowl to Skye and Skye took a small portion of salad. Mom finished cutting the lasagna and scooped an oversized portion onto everyone's plates. The girls ate their lasagna, and both had second helpings. Everyone enjoyed the special supper and emptied their plates. "Bella, do you and Skye want to go and try to contact Zenny and arrange a time to meet her back in Krystal while I do the dishes? When you are done communicating with her, I would like to meet back here so we can work together and hatch our new plan to get Skye and the egg back home safely," Mom laughed at her own pun.

"Good one Mom," groaned Bella, "I love your jokes. We will go contact Zenny and then we will come back down so we can 'hatch' a plan," laughed Bella. Bella and Skye went upstairs and moved the mattress to check on the egg. It was in the middle of a flashing cycle. When the cycle was over, Bella opened her dresser and stretched to reach the very back of her underwear drawer. She got out an old box that had a picture of a shoe on the side. When she opened the box, it was full of socks. Bella reached into the box and got out a large pair of white socks. "Do you like my hiding spot for my crystals from Krystal?" Bella asked with a grin.

"Yes, it's a great hiding spot, I had no idea what you were doing," said Skye. Bella got out the large pink crystal. "That crystal is beautiful, and so large. I hope we can contact Zenny with it," said Skye in awe.

"This crystal has allowed me to talk to Zenny many times, so if she is available, we should be able to talk to her tonight. She is going to be so excited when she hears her baby has started flashing and is going to be born soon. Let's get started," said Bella. Bella held the crystal tightly in her hand and it began to warm, then glow. Skye watched in amazement. Bella continued to concentrate on the crystal and Zenny. Bella thought she could hear sounds of dragons in the keep but there was no sign of Zenny answering her. "We might have to try again later," said Bella.

"Could we please keep trying, I know Zenny is waiting for this call," Skye looked hopefully toward Bella. Bella went to her shoe box and got the other pink crystal to increase the power of her communication. Bella held both large pink crystals and started to concentrate, the crystals began to warm in her hands, then they began to glow. Bella kept her concentration centred on Zenny.

Bella suddenly heard Zennys voice; it was very faint and sounded far away. "Zenny, it's Bella. Your precious egg is safe and very beautiful. It began to glow and flash today. The flashing looked like little lightning bolts; it was amazing. Your baby must be very special. When should I open the passageway for Skye to bring the egg to you?" Bella asked anxiously.

"Bella my friend, tomorrow we go to battle with our enemies. You can not send Skye through tomorrow. The danger would be too great, but I will meet you in the morning of the following day at the same time and place that Chief Tyee sent Skye to meet you. Warrior and I will both try to be there to meet Skye and bring our baby safely back to the keep," Zenny explained.

"Please be careful in the battle Zenny, your baby and I really need you to keep yourself safe!" emphasized Bella.

"I wish you were with me, Circee, we fight well together. Princess Alli will be my rider, and my harness will be filled with green crystals so I will be a force to be reckoned with. I will not do anything dangerous because I have a lot to look forward to and to live for with my little golden egg about to hatch. I also hope someday I will see you again, Great Circee," Zenny said with much admiration. Bella could feel the crystals begin to cool in her hands.

"I love you Zenny," Bella yelled with tears in her eyes at the thought of her friend going to battle tomorrow. Bella didn't know if her friend had heard her or not, but she certainly hoped she had. Bella continued to cry as she put the crystals away in the box at the back of her underwear drawer. Skye was also on the verge of crying; she was so worried about her friends and her home. The girls went downstairs, and Mom couldn't believe her eyes when she saw them both crying.

"What has happened?" asked Mom with concern in her voice. Both girls looked at Mom and started to cry even harder. Mom wrapped them both in a hug and waited for their tears to stop so she could find out what was going on. After several minutes their sobs subsided, and Skye began to speak.

"My village, and Zenny, are going to battle tomorrow," Skye said between sobs. This made Bella cry harder again and bury her head back in mom's shoulder.

"That explains the tears, you are scared for your friends and also feel guilty for not being there to help," said Mom, understanding perfectly. Bella nodded her head up and down with it still resting against Mom's shoulder. "From what you told me about the last battle your friends have a lot of skills and some strong magic on their side. So, I think that they will be triumphant in this battle too," Mom said encouragingly.

"Do you really think so, Mom?" asked Bella. She was saddened by the thought of her friends in battle. "I won't be there to use the red healing crystals if someone gets hurt."

Skye was nodding her agreement, "Bella saved Bade all by herself when he was injured in the last battle to save our purple life crystal from being stolen. She is a hero. Who will help if someone gets hurt this time?" asked Skye worriedly.

"Who else knows how to use the crystals?" Mom wondered. The girls looked at each other.

"I saw Chief Tyee use the crystals when he and I were saving Alli after she was hurt," remembered Bella. "Alli also knew a lot about the scrolls and crystals when she helped me get back home to you Mom, but I didn't ever see her use the healing crystals."

"She has had a lot of time to train since you have come home, so I'm sure she will be able to use the crystals if she needs to," said Mom confidently.

"You're right Mom, they are going to be okay tomorrow," Bella said, reassuring herself.

"They will be triumphant," said Skye as she said a prayer for her village. "Now let's focus on planning how to get the golden egg safely back to Krystal."

"Great idea Skye, let's start 'hatching' our plan," laughed Mom. The girls groaned at Mom's repeated joke and then they all got started throwing out ideas about how to get the precious egg home.

Chapter 14

Exciting news

Zenny was anxiously waiting for Warrior's return and when she saw him, she rushed to his side and began to explain about her exciting communication with Bella about their baby. "Our precious golden egg began to flash today, they will be sending the egg back home to us the day after tomorrow, at the same time Chief Tyee sent Skye to Bella," explained Zenny. Warrior was so excited he reared onto his hind legs and let out a big squeal. He wrapped Zenny lovingly in his wings and held her close. Chief Tyee smiled warmly at them both. "Good news about your egg?" inquired Chief Tyee.

"The best news," communicated Warrior, "our egg began to flash, and Skye will be bringing it home the day after tomorrow at the same time you sent Skye to Bella."

"That is great news, We will just have to win this battle quickly tomorrow so you two can rest before the baby arrives. I am very excited to see what type of precious baby will emerge from that beautiful golden egg." said Chief Tyee excitedly. He finished getting food and water for the dragons with extra for Zenny and Warrior after their long day. He then headed to the house to wait for Bade's return so the three of them could begin planning the strategy for the morning's battle. Chief Tyee entered the house with a big grin on his face. "Why are you smiling?" asked Alli, "it seems quite out of place when we have to go into a battle tomorrow."

"I know something you don't know," laughed Chief Tyee at his sister. "I bet you can't guess either," teased Chief Tyee.

"I don't know what you are getting on about, but I strongly suggest that you tell me immediately or I will hold the supper I have prepared for you for ransom or maybe even just eat it myself," laughed Alli.

"No, No, you couldn't possibly do that," chuckled Chief Tyee. "I will tell you. The brave Circee Bella was in contact with Zenny and the precious egg has started to flash."

"Ahhhhhhhhhh," screamed Alli as she ran to hug her brother, "that is wonderful but how will we get it home with the battle tomorrow?" asked Alli with great concern in her voice.

"Don't worry, Zenny arranged for them to come back the morning after the battle so they will be safe. We just have to end this tomorrow." said the Chief confidently. Just then Bade was back, with a quick knock on the front door while he let himself in.

"Hi everyone, are you ready to plan tomorrow's battle," asked Bade seriously.

"We know something you don't know," laughed Alli. Chief Tyee couldn't help but join in his sister's contagious laughter.

"What are you two up to?" inquired Bade with a smile.

"Circee communicated with Zenny, the egg began to glow this afternoon and Skye is bringing the precious egg home the day after tomorrow," said Alli excitedly.

"Oh, that is spectacular," said Bade as he hugged Alli, picking her up and swinging her around off her feet. "I can't wait to meet that precious dragon."

"I think you just wanted to hug my sister," chuckled Chief Tyee.

"Yes, that too, there's always that," said Bade smiling lovingly at Alli.

"I've made us a delicious meal, let's eat now and discuss the strategy for tomorrow's battle." said Alli on her way to the stone table to set out the food.

"I can't wait, I'm starving," said Chief Tyee.

"Me too," said Bade as he followed Alli towards the table.

"You two go wash your hands while I get the food on the table, and then we will eat," said Alli. The two men went to the bathroom to wash up and Alli got the delicious smelling food onto the table. The three of them talked about different plans for the battle tomorrow and ended up combining their strategies and ideas. It was a great combined plan to defeat their enemies as fast as possible. Chief Tyee wasn't worried about their victory against 30 people, but he was very worried about possibly hurting the children that Bade had seen in the enemies' camp when he had been scouting. The three friends finished their meal and they all got ready to go out and complete their tasks. Bade's task was to talk to the villagers about tomorrow's battle plan, it was a big task, so he left quickly after giving Alli a kiss. Alli's job was to go to the keep and make sure the dragons were all ready for tomorrow's battle, and make sure the trainers gave early rations in the morning. Chief Tyee was headed back to the 'dungeon' to try and find out the weaknesses of their enemies from their large smelly captive. He hoped their prisoner would cooperate. Warrior sensed that Chief Tyee was arriving and quickly left the keep and went to meet him outside. Alli waved to Chief Tyee when she reached the path to the keep, and he kept going towards the armories.

"See you later Alli", called Chief Tyee when they parted ways. Alli on her way to the keep and Chief Tyee on his way to the 'dungeon'. "Hi Warrior, you sensed us coming, did you?" asked Chief Tyee, patting the dragon's shoulder. "Congratulations again on your egg starting to flash, that's super exciting. We must get through the battle and then we are home free and safe once more. We will be ready to welcome your baby." The two friends walked quickly together up to the armouries to talk to the prisoner. They both had their minds on the golden egg and what it would mean for the future of the village. When they approached the armories, they could see the guards still doing a great job of guarding the entrance to the 'dungeon'. "Hi men, said Chief Tyee, has it all been quiet on your watch?"

"Yes Sir," said the first guard, "no action to report, also the prisoner has remained silent."

"Well, I'm here to see if I can change that, and possibly find out some helpful information to help us in tomorrow's battle. Warrior, you help the men guard the front of the 'dungeon' so they can have a short supper break while I interrogate the prisoner." Chief Tyee went inside and stood by the smelly man. The man looked up with fear showing on his face when he saw Chief Tyee. "Tell me your name?" commanded Chief Tyee. The man remained silent. "Tell me your name", he said again, "you must realize you are at a disadvantage, as it's five men and a dragon against you."

"I am Simon, but if I talk to you, the leader of my camp will kill me and if he doesn't, the leader of my tribe most certainly will, and he will also torture my wife and sons. So, you see sir, it would be better if you just killed me and spared my family from torture," said Simon with a single silent tear running down his face.

"Your leader is truly barbaric if he would torture anyone, let alone a child," stated Chief Tyee with disgust. Chief Tyee then sat down on the floor in front of the smelly man. "Tell me, what does your leader have against you and your family Simon?" asked Chief Tyee. Simon looked into the kind face of the chief and decided to confide in him, he didn't have anything to lose anyway.

"The great and powerful leader of my people thinks he can have or conquer anything he wants. My wife is very beautiful, and honorable, she rejected his advances when she was betrothed to me. This angered our leader so much that we have been in service to him ever since. It was that or die. We must do whatever he says or still we risk death. It is not a good life, but it is the only one we have. My wife and I have thought of trying to escape with our children, but if we were caught, I can only imagine our terrible fate, it would be worse than death," expressed Simon hanging his head defeatedly.

"So, it was your children our scouts saw when they located your camp on the far west side of our territory?" inquired Chief Tyee. Simon looked worriedly at Chief Tyee.

"Then you have found our camp," said Simon sadly. "Those were my children; we were the only parents forced to bring our children on this expedition. My family was sent to be the slaves for the whole raiding party. We have been commanded to do the bidding of the leader of this expedition, Grindle. That is precisely what I was doing when you captured me, Grindle had shot one of his best arrows into the trees back at our last camp and I was sent to retrieve it. You captured me on the way, so I don't even have the arrow." said Simon defeatedly.

"Do you want to go back to your tribe, or would you like to help us defeat them, so that you and your family could live in peace here with our tribe?" suggested Chief Tyee. Simon looked at Chief Tyee hopefully.

"You would do that for us, you don't even know us," stated Simon.

"Any man that would die before he put his family in any danger is a quality man," said Chief Tyee. Simon smiled for the first time since his capture.

"I would do anything for my family. How can I help you to save your people, your dragons and my precious family?" asked Simon.

"First, you can start by telling me what your leader's mission is. What is he trying to accomplish?" asked Chief Tyee.

"Grindle has been told to seek out and capture dragons. We didn't even know for sure if dragons were real until we got here and saw the magnificent beasts flying overhead. Grindle thought it would be too dangerous to try capture a full-sized dragon, so he had the idea of stealing four eggs but since you went on alert after we took the first two, we have not been able to get anywhere near the eggs to get the other two. Grindle has also been stealing food and livestock to feed the raiding party," confessed Simon.

"What are the weaknesses of your raiding party?" asked Chief Tyee. Does Grindle have any fears that we could play upon and hopefully get him to surrender?"

"We are all superstitious and Grindle is afraid of anything that flies. He seems especially afraid of dragons, so you already have the advantage. He is really a dangerous man though, and if he is afraid of something his solution is to kill it," said Simon sadly. "That puts everyone in great danger."

"That does make him a very dangerous man," said Chief Tyee. "We have already made a battle strategy, but we will have to come up with an extra plan to get your wife and children to safety before the battle begins." The two men sat and talked until they agreed on a plan to save Simon's family from their horrible life of slavery. Chief Tyee alerted the guards that they could untie Simon but to stay on guard in case he tried to escape. The guards followed Chief Tyee's orders and untied Simon and gave him a drink of water. They all left the armouries and Chief Tyee sealed the door with his magic.

Simon couldn't believe his eyes when the hill closed as easily as it had opened. The group started walking towards the keep, first the two guards, then Simon, followed by the other two guards. Chief Tyee and the mighty Warrior completed the group. When they got back to the keep, Chief Tyee went in and readied an empty stall and then instructed the guards to continue to watch the prisoner closely inside the stall. The loyal guards assumed their posts with two in the stall with Simon and two at the entrance to the stall holding their weapons ready for anything.

"Warrior, you and Zenny need to sleep, you two have a really big couple of days coming up," said Chief Tyee patting the giant dragon's shoulder. Warrior nuzzled Chief Tyee and went into the keep to find Zenny and settle in for a short sleep before tomorrow's battle. Chief Tyee went towards his house to talk to Alli about the new development. When he entered the house, he found Alli practicing using the crystals to transform rocks that she had collected into arrows for the battle. "What a great use of your practice skills preparing arrows for our brave villagers to use in the battle," said Chief Tyee admiringly.

"I really wanted to practice and tried to think of a useful thing to practice with. My first attempt just looked like a rock with a nose not an arrow at all, it took me three tries to get it working so that I could make what I was trying to. Circee must be really gifted to have been able to accomplish so much in such a short time. I wish she was here right now, We could really use her skills," said Alli with a sigh.

"The great Circee was a very brave and skilled warrior, she worked very hard during her training, and even now she is keeping Zenny's egg safe from our enemies. I may never know why she fell into our land, but I will be forever grateful that she did," said Chief Tyee fondly.

"How did your interrogation of the prisoner go?" questioned Alli.

"It did not go at all how I was expecting it to go. It turns out our prisoner's name is Simon, and he is a slave to the leader of his tribe. He, along with his wife and two sons, were sent on this mission as a slave for the leader of their raiding party. He was the only person forced to bring his wife and children. His two children are the only ones in the camp. His wife and family would love a safe place to live where they are not slaves to the whims of a tyrant," said Chief Tyee angrily.

"Do you think we can trust him?" asked Alli worriedly.

"I don't know for sure, but he certainly seemed sincere when I was talking to him," said Chief Tyee. "I have left the guards posted on him for now and we will see how he behaves after we rescue his family."

"You are a pretty solid judge of character my brother, I am hoping he becomes an asset to our village," said Alli reassuringly. Just then, Bade was back with a quick knock on the door as he opened it.

"All went well getting the livestock put away, Old Calon, even had some goats out to pasture, it was quite the round up," laughed Bade.

"I'm so glad you were there to help him," said Alli chuckling, "poor Old Calon might have been there all night."

"How did it go getting the dragons ready and interrogating the prisoner?" inquired Bade.

"The dragons went really well, they are ready for tomorrow, I think Zenny and Warrior might have other things on their mind though," smiled Alli.

"The interrogation did not go as expected," said Chief Tyee.

"Oh no, you made Warrior eat him," laughed Bade.

"No," smiled Chief Tyee, "but we may have a new family joining our community."

"You really need to explain how that smelly man is going to join our community and be an asset to anything," said Bade angrily. "They come into our land and steal our dragons' eggs and then they want to move in, sounds suspicious to me."

"Bade, I know that you are on edge going into battle tomorrow, but Simon has been a slave in his own country for almost 15 years. He really wants to leave his homeland to save his family from their horrible life," said Chief Tyee convincingly.

"I trust your judgement my friend, you have always led us with the best of intentions," said Bade. The two men shook hands and hugged; it was time to focus on the battle. Dawn was coming quickly.

Chapter 15

The Rescue

Two hours before the sun rose Chief Tyee and Bade went to the keep to get Simon, they found him kneeling in prayer while the guards watched him closely.

"Simon, it is time to go rescue your family," said Chief Tyee softly. Simon raised his head and smiled at Chief Tyee.

"I am ready," he said getting up. Chief Tyee sent two of the guards home to prepare for the battle and kept two of the guards with him. They quietly discussed the plan as they walked so that everyone would know their role in the rescue mission. All the men were very confident in their assigned jobs. When they got closer to the camp, they all were silent and walked stealthily toward Simon's tent where his family was sleeping. Simon's tent was on the edge of the group, away from the main tents. This symbolized his family's lack of value to their tribe. As they approached the tent, Simon could hear his wife crying and he hurried faster to find out what was wrong. When Simon moved the flap of the tent, his wife gasped in fright. Simon quickly put his hand over his wife's mouth to silence her. The other men waited outside on guard in case any of the other enemies woke up. Simon quickly explained to his wife that they were escaping and he and his wife each picked up a sleeping child keeping them wrapped in their blankets and quietly exited the tent. They hurried as quickly as they could away from the camp. The guards, Bade, and Chief Tyee followed quickly behind them. The oldest child in his fathers' arms woke up and quickly hugged his father.

"Put me down Papa, I can run," he whispered. Simon put his son down and took the smaller child from his wife. The youngest child was still asleep and, despite the cool night air, remained that way until they were far away from the camp and Simon began to talk quietly to his wife.

"I was captured by these men, Olga, but they are good men, they have agreed to let us live here and start a new life without being slaves anymore. Our children will not have to live in constant fear. We will be free," Simon said with joy. The small child in Simon's arms began to stir.

"Will I be free too, papa?" the small child asked.

"Yes, my beautiful child, you will be free too." Simon said as he kissed his child on the head. His child smiled up at him and wrapped their arms tightly around his neck. When they were getting back close to the keep, they only had about a half hour before dawn. Chief Tyee knew they had to hurry to be back to the clearing by dawn to get ready for the battle. He instructed his two guards to take the family to the keep and guard them in the stall that Simon had been using. The guards and the family went towards the keep while Bade and Chief Tyee went to the house. The lights were already on, so Alli must be awake and preparing for the battle. When they entered the house, they found Alli practicing with the orange crystals. She was in the process of disappearing right before their eyes.

"Now you see her, then you don't," laughed Chief Tyee.

"I really prefer to see her," laughed Bade. "Alli, where are you?"

"I am right beside you," she said as she let go of the one orange crystal and started to reappear. Bade jumped. Chief Tyee laughed.

"Hey, don't scare me like that," he said laughing as he gave Alli a kiss on the lips.

"How did the rescue go?" asked Alli. "It must have gone well, or you wouldn't be back so quickly."

"It actually went seamlessly, everything Simon told us was accurate. His wife and kids left with nothing more than the clothes on their backs and were very happy to be leaving, so their lives must have been pretty bad. I heard the youngest child ask if they were going to be free too, and you should have seen the joy on their little face when Simon told the child yes," said Chief Tyee.

"They are very lucky that you captured Simon," said Alli smiling. She patted her brother on the arm. "You are a great and kind man," she said to Chief Tyee. "I have the morning meal ready as well, we will need our strength for battle. Yes Bade, before you ask, there's extra strong warm cocoa." Alli and Bade smiled at each other. Bade couldn't believe how lucky he was to have a betrothed who cared so much about him. The three of them hurriedly ate their morning meal and then busied themselves, getting their armor on and loading up their pouches with crystals to be ready for the battle. Alli and Chief Tyee got extra green crystals ready for Zenny and Warrior because they would be front and centre during the fight and could help transform their enemies. In less than half an hour they were walking towards the keep to get their dragons ready and head for the clearing before dawn fully broke. Inside the keep Simon and his family were sitting quietly in the stall with the two guards watching them. When Simon saw Chief Tyee, he rose to his feet.

"I would like to come with you into battle, I owe you so much already, I would like to start to try and repay you. I know where Grindle's tent is, and I know where they are keeping the dragon eggs. I would be honoured if you would let me help you to win this battle and retrieve the eggs." said Simon emotionally.

"Very well, you can come and fight, I will take any advantage that I can get. I will assign one of our soldiers to stay with you to help you find the eggs and get them to safety," said Chief Tyee.

Chapter 16

Extreme Battle

The group set off with their mighty dragons toward the clearing to join the others. The group was very quiet, all their minds focused on the battle ahead. When they arrived at the clearing, Chief Tyee was surprised by how many villagers had come to help. He was so proud of all of them.

"Hello everyone," Chief Tyee said, smiling at his tribe. "We will end this battle quickly with so many of you here to help. Thank you for your bravery and support."

They reviewed the battle strategy with the group and broke into four units, one unit attacking from each side. Chief Tyee took the east side, attacking from the front. Alli took the north side with her battalion. Bade took the south side, and one of the trusted guards was to lead the attack from the west. Simon and the villager who was assigned to help him save the eggs stayed with Chief Tyee to rush in from the front and retrieve them.

The guard leading the west attack and his battalion set off first and would have a half an hour head start to get into position because they had the farthest to go. In a quarter hour Alli and Bade would set off with their battalions to get into position. Chief Tyee would then ready his troop and get into position. When Chief Tyee was ready, he would fly into the air and begin the advance. They had all been instructed to wait for Chief Tyee and Warrior to rise into the air and then they all knew to charge with all their might.

They said their goodbyes and assembled into their units. The trusted guard set off for the west side at a swift pace followed closely by his brave battalion. After a quarter hour had passed, Bade gave Alli an extra kiss and hug. They both set off to ready their troops into position and await Chief Tyee's signal to attack. Chief Tyee waited the quarter hour and then began to move forward to get his troop into position. They moved swiftly and determinedly under the cover of the last shadows of the morning. When they reached an area within view of the camp they stopped and readied their weapons, prepared their dragons and checked their armor one last time. At last, it was time. The sun was rising and so was Chief Tyee on his mighty dragon, Warrior. As he rose into the sky above the treeline, he thrust his huge sword up into the air and all of his troops who had been awaiting the signal began to advance. Chief Tyee got to the camp first, one of the enemies saw him coming and sounded the alarm. It was chaos after that with everyone running out of their tents, weapons in hand and attacking Chief Tyee's troops. Bade and his battalion arrived next and began their attack. Alli and her troop and the troop from the west arrived at the same time, blocking the enemy's retreat in all directions. Chief Tyee had made way for Simon and his guard to get into the tent containing the eggs. He had strategically sent in his warriors to block a path for them. The guard and Simon advanced quickly to the tent containing the eggs but only one egg was there.

"Grindle," cursed Simon quietly under his breath. Simon gave the egg to the guard. "Grindle must have taken the other egg to his tent, I'm going after it," Simon said determinedly. "You take this egg to safety."

"Stay safe Simon," said the guard as he began to run the egg back to the safety of the keep. Simon began to advance towards Grindle's tent just as Grindle was trying to sneak out the back carrying a large sack with the egg inside. He saw that Grindle had his powerful bow and a quiver full of his murderous barbed arrows in his hand. Simon watched helplessly as Grindle charged directly towards Alli, with a loaded arrow in his powerful bow. Simon took off running as fast as he could to try to help Alli and retrieve the dragon egg from the cruel Grindle.

Chief Tyee was winning in his quadrant and had either turned his enemies into mice or had them captured and tied up. He began moving towards the north to help Alli and her troops defeat the enemies in their area. As Chief Tyee turned toward Alli and Zenny, he saw them transforming some of their enemies into mice with the green crystals and smiled. Then out of the corner of his eye, he saw Simon running toward Alli. He saw the large man drawing back his bow and aiming it directly towards her. Chief Tyee broke into a sprint, screaming for Alli to watch out, not believing the horror unfolding before him.

Grindle shot his arrow and it hit Alli in the thigh. She fell from Zenny's back and went down screaming in agony. Zenny turned and saw Grindle with his bow reloaded and pointed again directly at Alli, who was still writhing in agony on the ground. Zenny let out a ferocious roar and ran straight toward Grindle, blocking Alli from the murderer. When Grindle heard the dragon's ferocious roar and saw the mighty dragon advancing on him, he changed the trajectory of his arrow and fired at Zenny. The arrow pierced through her thick hide and embedded itself deeply in her chest. Zenny let out a blood curdling cry of pain before collapsing onto the ground.

In Grindle's distraction with the dragon, he hadn't seen Simon approaching. Simon raised his sword and plunged it through the evil Grindle. Grindle instantly fell to the ground, dead, never again able to cause hurt or destruction to anyone or anything. Simon grabbed the bag containing the precious egg and swiftly rushed to Zenny's aid. Chief Tyee was the first to arrive at Alli's side followed quickly by an anxious Bade. Alli was ashen lying quietly on the ground, Bade cradled her head in his lap as a tear rolled down his cheek. Tyee had already gotten the red crystals from his pouch and handed two to Bade and kept two for himself. He checked Alli's thigh and saw that the murderous barbed arrow had pierced the top of her thigh and the tip was partially exposed right out the other side of her leg. Bade was holding the crystals against Alli's chest and they were starting to glow. Chief Tyee cut the arrow in half and decided to pull the barbed point through her leg in an effort to minimize the damage to Alli's muscles. Alli screamed with pain when Chief Tyee removed the arrow and then she fainted against Bade. It was Bade's turn to scream.

"Alli, Alli, Alli," he cried more loudly each time, "stay with us. You are not allowed to die. You are only allowed to live for a very long time with me," Bade said commanding her to obey.

As soon as Chief Tyee had the arrow removed, he grabbed his crystals and felt them warm in his hands and begin to glow. He concentrated very hard on healing Alli's leg and saving his beloved sister. She had lost so much blood; it was coloring the battlefield all around her with the crimson color of her life. Finally, with much intense concentration by Chief Tyee, the blood flow slowed and then stopped completely.

"Bade, use your crystals, and keep healing Alli," commanded Chief Tyee. "I must help Zenny." Bade went into action mode and began to focus on the crystals. Chief Tyee could see Bade's crystals begin to glow brighter and knew he could confidently leave his sister in her betrothed's capable hands. He hurried over to Zenny to inspect her wound. Simon was already there putting pressure around the arrow to help stop the bleeding. Warrior was at Zenny's side with his wing over her. He was making soft cooing sounds. The other dragons had encircled them and were making a humming vibration.

"Oh Zenny, you were very brave. Thank you for saving Alli. We have to heal you now; please try and stay still so we can get this arrow out of you as safely as possible," Chief Tyee instructed her. He retrieved the healing crystals from out of his pouch and held them against Zenny's wound. He felt them begin to warm and then saw them glow. He was concentrating on healing Zenny with every ounce of his strength and will.

"Simon, what is the best way to remove this awful arrow?" asked Chief Tyee. Simon had been watching in amazement as Chief Tyee used the crystals. The blood flow from the wound had slowed to a trickle right before his eyes. Magical healing stones were something he had only heard told of in children's stories, he couldn't believe they were real.

"Grindle had the worst arrows, there will be many sharp barbs and to remove them quickly will cause much damage. I have had practice removing them from hunted game and the best luck I have had is to place my finger into the wound and cover the barbs with the hollows of large feathers and then the barbs don't catch on the way out and cause more damage," said Simon with concern in his voice.

Chief Tyee called out to his tribesmen, "Hurry and find as many feathers as you can! We must use their hollow shafts to cover the barbs on the arrow in Zenny so we can remove it with the least damage and save her life." Every available tribesperson raced to find feathers on the arrows that were littered around the campsite after the battle.

Simon raced toward Grindle's tent hoping he hadn't used all the white feathers from the giant egrets yet. Simon had been forced to gather many feathers for him before the expedition set out. He really hoped he would find them unused in Grindle's tent, so he could help Zenny. When he got to the tent, he quickly rummaged through everything until he found the satchel that he had used to gather the great white feathers. It was still three quarters full, thank goodness Grindle was lazy and hadn't used them yet to make his arrows. Simon ran with the satchel as quickly as he could back to Zenny.

Chief Tyee had stopped the bleeding from the wound and Zenny's breathing was easier when Simon returned with the feathers. Simon cut the tip from the first feather and handed it to Chief Tyee.

"No Simon. You know what you are feeling for, and you will be able to cover the barbs more quickly, I will cut the tips for you," said Chief Tyee solemnly.

"It would be my honour Sir," said Simon. He reached for the first feather and slid his finger along with the feather into the wound to find the deepest barb. Zenny let out a small groan and Warrior released a deep growl of protection over his precious mate. Simon was afraid of Warrior but reassured him he was trying to help, and he kept gently working to cover the barbs one by one with the white feathers. After the fourth feather, Zenny's wound began to bleed again. Chief Tyee had to concentrate intently on the healing crystals and one of his trusted villagers continued to cut the feather tips for Simon. After twelve barbs were covered, Simon announced he had covered them all.

"I will prepare Warrior and Zenny for the arrow's removal," said Chief Tyee with concern. He bent close to where Warrior and Zenny's heads touched and whispered that they were going to remove the arrow and that he needed them both to remain strong and courageous. Everything was going to be alright.

Just then Bade arrived with news that Alli was awake but very weak, she was being cared for by the villagers so that he could help with Zenny.

"Thank you for the update," said Chief Tyee, "you are just in time. Please get as many healing crystals as you can handle and start concentrating on healing Zenny's wound while I remove this arrow."

Bade did as he was told and held four crystals in each hand; he was already exhausted from helping to heal Alli, but he would do whatever it took to help heal Zenny. The crystals began to warm and then glow.

Chief Tyee waited until the crystals were glowing brightly and there wasn't even a dribble of blood flowing from the wound. He then spoke to Zenny, "On the count of three I will remove the arrow: One, Two, Three." Chief Tyee gave a mighty heave and the arrow slipped free from Zenny's chest. Zenny was motionless and her eyes fluttered closed, Warrior let out an ear-piercing roar followed by the roars of the dragons around the circle.

Simon had covered every barb, so no more damage was done inside Zenny, but she had passed out from the pain and loss of blood. Chief Tyee quickly grabbed more healing crystals and began to concentrate on stopping the blood that was pouring from Zenny's chest. It didn't take long to get the bleeding stopped and the wound on its way to healing but Zenny's breathing was shallow. They needed to get her back to the keep.

Chapter 17

After the Battle

"**B**ade, we need to get Zenny back to the keep, and we need to help any of our injured villagers. Take your crystals and check if any of our brave villagers need any medical attention. I am going to stay with Zenny and keep using the crystals to try restore her health. She has lost a lot of blood and will need great care and attention to heal," said Chief Tyee worriedly. Bade reluctantly did as he was told. He wanted to help Zenny and Alli, but he knew he had a duty to the brave villagers who had volunteered to come out to help fight their enemies today. Their tribe had been victorious in the battle and the brave villagers had forced their enemies into surrendering.

Bade rushed to help heal his people. He helped with six arrow wounds, set a broken leg, and tended to many burns. The burns resulted from the enemy throwing coals from their burning campfires at the villagers and these coals had inflicted much pain. Bade was completely exhausted when he finally returned to Alli. She was looking a little better and was taking a sip of water when he knelt down beside her.

"You are looking a little stronger, my beautiful Alli," said Bade lovingly with as big of a smile as he could muster. "We need to get you home so you can recover." Alli returned his smile with a weak smile of her own. Suddenly Simon came running up to Bade and Alli.

"Do you need a stretcher for Alli?" he asked with concern in his voice. "I have designed one for Zenny using some of the tents and the dragons will be able to lift her and carry her back to the keep with it."

"Is Zenny going to be okay?" asked Alli with tears welling up in her eyes "She sacrificed herself to save me."

"Your brother is doing everything he can to heal her," Simon reassured her, "and I have been praying for her and all of you."

"Alli will ride back with me and then I will send my dragon back to help carry Zenny," stated Bade as he went to communicate this with his dragon and talk with Chief Tyee. Bade found Chief Tyee with the crystals still glowing in his hands and sweat dripping from his forehead. His eyes were closed in intense concentration. "Tyee my Chief," said Bade quietly so as not to startle his friend. Chief Tyee opened his eyes. "Simon has almost gotten a stretcher made from tents ready to transport Zenny back to the keep, all the villagers have been tended to, and Alli is a little stronger."

"That is all good news, we will be able to fly Zenny back to the keep and I can keep tending her there," said Chief Tyee on the edge of exhaustion.

"What do you want to be done with the ten prisoners that we have?" asked Bade patiently.

"Take them to one of the farmer's corrals, keep them tied up and post guards around the clock until we can decide what to do with them," Chief Tyee said angrily. Bade left to follow his instructions. Chief Tyee stayed with Zenny and kept the crystals glowing. Simon and the villagers brought the huge stretcher to place it beside the large dragon. Simon began rolling up the edge of the tents along her back. "Whatever you are doing you had better be gentle," threatened Chief Tyee.

"I know a way of getting this underneath her that requires us to move her very little. It will be much better than trying to lift her," said Simon compassionately. "I used to use this trick on my grandmother to change her bed sheets before she died. It was the gentlest way I could find to move my beloved grandma and I will be just as gentle with this amazing dragon," reassured Simon. Chief Tyee relaxed a little while Simon and the guards worked on getting the huge makeshift stretcher ready. Finally, it was time to move Zenny onto the stretcher. Simon had given everyone instructions on how to move Zenny first upward so that they could get the rolled-up portion of the stretcher under her and then gently roll her backward just far enough to pull the rolled edge of the stretcher from under her. Then when it was unrolled on the other side, she would be completely on the stretcher. Chief Tyee stayed at Zenny's chest with the healing crystals still glowing. Simon guarded Zenny's head and ten people gently pushed her body up and five additional people rolled the tent stretcher lump halfway under her body. Zenny let out a moan when they rested her body back down on the lump. Warrior growled. The people quickly changed sides and repeated the process. When completed, Zenny was centred on the stretcher and ready to be flown home. Bade's dragon had returned and was standing beside Warrior at Zenny's head. Chief Tyee remained at Zenny's chest with the healing crystals glowing. Simon and the other villagers quickly arranged the dragons around the stretcher and then coordinated a rider for each dragon. They tied the stretcher ropes securely to each dragon's harness. Chief Tyee told Simon it was okay to ride Bade's dragon, but only after he had communicated this request to Warrior and Warrior had received permission from the other dragon to allow Simon to ride. It was Simon's first time mounting a dragon and he was really struggling. Bade's dragon had to lay right down before Simon could mount, and Warrior snorted his disbelief. Chief Tyee smiled for the first time in a long time at the dragon's making fun of Simon.

Chief Tyee looked at the crew and commanded, "On the count of three, lift with all your might and we will rise smoothly into the air as one large unit. Ready? One, Two, Three!" The sound of the dragon's wing beats catching the air at the same time was almost deafening, but their ascent was smooth and precise and soon they had Zenny flying through the air on the giant makeshift stretcher. The dragons were able to fly remarkably quickly, considering the enormous weight they were carrying. They could see the keep in no time. When they landed, Bade was there readying a stall for Zenny. He had the help of the guards as well as Simon's children. They had a soft bed of fresh straw waiting for the injured dragon. The dragon team carrying Zenny could barely fit through the door and a couple of them scraped their wings, but they managed to get Zenny laid down gently on her soft, fresh bed.

Chief Tyee quickly dismounted, ran to Zenny and got out his crystals; despite his exhaustion he had them glowing on her chest before the other riders had even dismounted.

"Bade, how is Alli, and who is with her?" asked Tyee worriedly.

"Simon's wife and one of the guards are with Alli, she is very weak, but she will be okay," said Bade with relief.

"Zenny hasn't gained consciousness yet, so I am pretty worried about her," said Chief Tyee sadly.

"She will pull through; I know she will," stated Bade assuredly. The trainers were already tending to the other dragons, washing their small wounds and burns as well as getting them food and water. Bade asked, "Tyee my chief what would be the greatest help for you what do you need me to do first."

"Please make sure that all of the dragons are cared for including the two eggs that we recovered. I saw the dapple dragon, Lucy, had a sore wing when we were flying back, and she doesn't communicate with any humans, so she needs some extra attention. Then please check on the guards that are with the new prisoners and make sure they have everything they need for the night. When you have finished those things, please stay with Alli, I will be staying here with Zenny," said Chief Tyee tiredly.

Bade patted Chief Tyee lovingly on the shoulder and left to complete his assigned tasks. Chief Tyee sat beside Zenny with the crystals glowing as brightly as he could manage, watching her breathing which was slow and steady. The night passed slowly for Chief Tyee and Warrior, there was no change in their beloved Zenny. When dawn finally came, Bade returned to the keep to care for Zenny so that Chief Tyee and Warrior could go to meet Skye and retrieve the precious golden egg.

Chapter 18

The Return

The day to travel back to Krystal and return the precious egg dawned in Bella's world with clear and sunny skies. This great bit of luck really helped with their plan because the highway going to the lake would be extra busy. They would have no trouble getting away from that persistent scientist with the extra traffic to help block him. Mom was up early preparing a meal for the girls and a bagged lunch for Skye to take with her through the passage. She had also purchased a couple of gifts, a warm hoodie in a bright pink color for Skye and a beautiful handmade solid steel knife in a leather case for Chief Tyee. Mom put the breakfast on the table and went to call the girls. When she entered their room, she found them ready for the big day and gazing happily at the egg which was putting on an entertaining show and flashing even faster than the day before.

"Good morning girls, are you ready for our big day?" Mom asked.

"Good morning Mom! We are very excited to get this egg home today, I'm sure the battle went well," said Bella. "Zenny will be happy to have her baby home."

"I am excited, but also a little scared to go back through the magical dark passage," said Skye apprehensively. Mom put her arm around Skye to comfort her.

"You are going to be fine; I have great faith in you, and I have faith in Chief Tyee, everything will be fine" said Mom reassuringly. Mom held out her hand and helped Skye up off the floor and the three of them went downstairs together.

Breakfast was eaten in an excited rush with much talking about the plan the three of them had devised and how they were going to slow down Jason, the annoying scientist, and keep him far away from Skye when she exited through the passage.

When breakfast was eaten, the girls went up to pack for the escape while Mom threw the dishes quickly into the dishwasher. They came back down, with the egg padded and wrapped and put into a carrier that strapped onto Skye's chest. They also had one of Bella's backpacks full of the wool Skye had purchased. Bella had given her the four chocolate bombs to give to Chief Tyee, Alli, Bade and of course one for Skye. They were tucked safely in the front pocket of the backpack. Mom had her surprise for Skye too, the beautiful pink hoodie. Skye loved it and tucked it into her backpack so that it wouldn't get dirty going through the tunnel.

"I have a gift for Chief Tyee as well if there is room in your very full backpack," laughed Mom as she looked at the bulging backpack full of wool.

"Of course, there is room," Skye said, taking the handcrafted knife from Mom and packing it carefully down the side of the backpack. The girls had to work together to close the zipper. The girls spent five minutes compressing the backpack and tugging at the zipper.

Bella laughed, "See, no problem."

The three of them all laughed together and had one final group hug.

"Do you for sure have everything?" asked Mom, "It's not really easy to come back."

The girls smiled and nodded, "Skye has the egg and I have my crystals, so I think that's everything that really matters," said Bella.

****Evasion**

The three of them went and got into their two cars as discreetly as possible. Bella and Skye were together in her car, and they waited for Mom to back out of the garage and then they were off to get the precious egg home. Mom drove right behind the girls with her car. Within minutes, Jason was visible in Mom's rear-view mirror. He was just a couple of cars back. Mom desperately hoped that their plan would work; she knew she would do whatever it took to keep the girls safe if it didn't.

As soon as they were out on the highway, Bella really sped up. Instead of following suit, Mom kept going as slowly as she could. Bella got further and further ahead as the traffic behind Mom started to back up. The traffic coming towards them was thick and no one could get past her. Their plan was working perfectly. Mom smiled to herself and kept a good watch on Jason's car two back. Mom continued at her slow speed with all the angry honking going on behind her for ten long minutes. The girls would have a huge head start.

After the ten minutes of agonizingly slow driving, mom took off like a shot towards the arranged meeting spot. Bella had driven as fast as she safely could and had made it to the secret location at the beach in no time. Bella and Skye ran towards the location of the secret passage. Bella got out her crystals and began to concentrate. She felt them begin to warm. Skye came and gave her a hug and when the egg brushed the crystals, they immediately began to glow brighter than Bella had ever seen before, and the tunnel appeared instantly.

"The baby must know it's going home and helped us out, I have never seen the passage appear that quickly before," said Bella in amazement.

Skye took a deep breath and hurried toward the tunnel to get the precious egg home. "Goodbye Bella, Thank you for everything," she said as she started to run into the passage.

"Goodbye my friend, I can't wait to hear about the hatching," Bella called after her.

Bella put her crystals away while she impatiently waited for the passage to close. When the passage closed, she would know Skye made it through to safety. Then she could concentrate on her own safety and get away before Jason found her. Suddenly she felt the earth give a shudder and the passage closed. Relief flooded through her. Bella carefully brushed away her footprints until she was back on the main path and then she started to sprint to her car. Mom was there waiting and handed Bella the garage door opener.

"Take the route we discussed and go right into the garage. Close it up tight. I will meet you at home after I run interference," Mom reminded Bella urgently.

Bella got into her little red car and sped away. Mom waited for Jason to show up at the beach, and sure enough not even two minutes after Bella had gotten away, he pulled in. Mom had been videoing him driving towards her and when he parked a couple of cars away, she waited for him to get out of his car.

"You have to quit stalking us, Jason. I will be taking this video along with my home security footage to request a restraining order," Mom growled at him.

"This is a public beach; I can be here if I want to be. Where are the girls?" Jason asked, looking down the beach, "Oh, and by the way, nice driving out there on the highway."

"If you are referring to my daughter and her friend, who you obviously are stalking, you won't find a trace of them here," said Mom confidently.

Jason began unloading equipment from his car to search the beach for any signs of the girls or any earthquake activity. He was also planning to do a thorough search for any radiation.

"We will see about that; I will be searching the beach for any evidence," said Jason defiantly.

Mom knew the girls had been careful and so she turned with a smile and went to her car. Bella had taken an extra long way home and would be there in fifteen minutes. Mom knew that Jason hadn't seen her, or he wouldn't still be here at the beach. Their plan had worked, she thought with relief. It really had been foolproof. Mom smiled.

Chapter 19

Safely Home

Chief Tyee and Warrior reluctantly left Zenny's side to go and meet Skye and the precious egg. They wanted Zenny to be with them to get her baby, but that was impossible. The two just kept hoping that Zenny would be okay.

The enemy had been defeated, and as such, the no-fly order was over. Warrior took to the sky and flew straight up with his rider. Chief Tyee felt the weight of worry being left behind and the excitement of the new baby beginning. Warrior flew swiftly to the meeting spot excited to retrieve his egg and meet his new baby. He landed at the site in record time.

Chief Tyee dismounted and waited with bated breath for the passage to open. Warrior was impatient and scratched at the ground. They stood at the meeting spot for almost an hour before Chief Tyee felt the ground quiver, and then watched with joy as the passage appeared. Two minutes later Skye ran through, breathless and cradling the precious egg. The tunnel quickly closed behind her. Skye looked around smiling, then her smile faded.

"Where's Zenny?" asked Skye, "I thought she would be here; her egg is amazing." Warrior hung his head. Skye looked questioningly at Chief Tyee.

"Let's get back," said Chief Tyee, "I will explain everything on the way." Skye hopped up onto Warrior with ease, quickly followed by the chief. Warrior took off, and Skye felt the egg move and then heard a crack.

"This egg is very anxious to meet its parents, I just heard the first crack," said Skye excitedly.

Warrior must have heard it too because he had already started to fly faster. Chief Tyee explained to Skye about the battle and that Zenny was seriously injured and had not yet regained consciousness. Tears were streaming down Skye's face when they landed; she dismounted from Warrior and ran as fast as she could to bring the egg to Zenny.

"Zenny, Zenny, wake up I have your baby," cried Skye as she hugged Zenny and then began unpacking the golden egg. As Skye unwrapped the egg, another small crack appeared in the shell. She laid the egg up against Zenny's chest for it to hatch.

Suddenly, a bright light originated from within the egg and blasted out through the cracks. Warrior and Chief Tyee had arrived just in time to witness the hatching. It was so bright, Skye needed to shield her eyes when the egg burst open. Bits of shell flew in all directions as Zenny and Warrior's precious baby entered the world.

As the beautiful black and gold baby reached out his claw and touched his Mom for the first time, there was a small lightning bolt shape of light emitted from the babies forehead. The lightning bolt hit Zenny and was absorbed into her chest. Zenny's eyes fluttered open. She lifted her head and cooed at her baby. Skye's tears turned from tears of sorrow to tears of joy, watching Zenny wake up and talk to her new baby. Warrior began to coo at the little dragon, and he put a wing around Zenny comfortingly.

The crowd in the barn let out a cheer at the baby's hatching and Zenny's amazing recovery. As Chief Tyee checked over Zenny, he couldn't believe his eyes; her wound was totally healed.

"Warrior, would you ask Zenny how she is, please?" asked Chief Tyee with disbelief, "and Skye, could you please go get the hatchling rations and tell the trainers to prepare some extra rations for Zenny, she will need them to start getting her strength back."

Skye hurried away while Chief Tyee continued his assessment of Zenny. The crowd in the barn continued to be amazed by Zenny's miraculous recovery. They were all enjoying watching the new baby getting to know its parents.

"Zenny says she feels strong, and that her heart is filled with joy having her baby back safely at her side," communicated Warrior. Chief Tyee was amazed by the miracle he had witnessed. Could the new baby really have healed its mother with just a touch?

As the chief pondered, one of the trainers brought one of the recovered eggs from yesterday to show it to Chief Tyee.

"Chief, I'm sorry to bother you," interrupted the trainer, but the egg that was cracked yesterday in the battle is not responding this morning. What should we do?"

Chief Tyee reached out for the egg, and felt that it was cool. He wondered whether it would be worth a try to let the new baby touch it. He brought the egg close to Zenny and her magical babe, holding the egg up toward him. The black and gold baby reached out his tiny talon and laid it against the side of the egg. The egg began to warm instantly, and a soft glow could be seen through the crack.

Chief Tyee was amazed at the baby dragon's powers. He couldn't wait to find out everything this amazing baby was going to be able to do.

"Take this egg to its Mother. It is going to hatch soon, so monitor it closely, this baby has had a rocky start. Oh, and please ask Skye to get some hatchling rations for this new baby too," instructed Chief Tyee.

The trainer hurried off smiling with the warm glowing egg, happy to go tell the good news to the egg's mother. Two hatchlings in one day what incredible news for the tribe.

Simon and his family sat and watched the baby dragon and his mom, Zenny. with awe and happiness. They had never seen dragons before, and baby dragons were especially endearing.

Not long after she had left, Skye arrived back with a trainer carrying hatchling rations for the baby and rations for Zenny and Warrior as well. Chief Tyee took the rations toward the baby and the little one let out an excited zzzzlurp sound that no one had heard before and when he began to eat, a small lightning bolt shot up out of his head scales and floated up and sparked Zenny. She looked startled at first and then nuzzled her little one as he kept eating.

"What was that?" Skye asked. "I noticed when his egg started to glow, it had lightning bolt patterns, but I didn't think he would be able to shoot them."

"I guess he has chosen his name, Lightning it is," laughed Chief Tyee. Zenny and the crowd all nodded in agreement. Warrior looked at his family with pride.

"He, you mean it's a boy?" asked Skye excitedly. Chief Tyee nodded and more cheers went through the crowd. "Congratulations on your new baby boy, Warrior and Zenny."

"Nice to meet you Lightning," said Bade, "Congratulations Warrior and Zenny. He's magnificent." Bade enjoyed watching the baby dragon.

"Okay everyone, let's give the new family some time to bond. I would like one of the trainers to keep a frequent eye on these three, they have had an eventful few days. The rest of you, please find something else to do. Skye, come with Bade and me up to the house to have a meal and exchange stories with Alli," said Chief Tyee.

A big grin split Skye's face. She said her goodbyes to Zenny and happily followed Chief Tyee. Skye was still wearing her backpack with all the gifts inside, so she was very excited to be invited into Chief Tyee's home to share them. When they got inside, Chief Tyee smelled delicious food and saw Alli sitting at the stone table. He heard singing coming from the kitchen and was confused about who it could be.

"Hello Alli, my beautiful sister, it is so nice to see you feeling stronger," Chief Tyee said happily. "Zenny has woken up and is feeling stronger as well. She has a new baby boy, Lightning, to tend to. He is an amazing mystery. Who, may I ask, is singing in my home?"

"What great news about Zenny and her new baby! That is Frieda singing, she heard what happened and arrived at daybreak and has been preparing food ever since," chuckled Alli.

It was Chief Tyee's and Bade's turn to smile, Frieda was one of the best cooks in the village. Frieda had heard them come in and came out to greet them.

"Hello, you can all go wash up while I put the morning meal on the table, I have left lunch and supper in the locker. I need to be getting home now, just send Skye to get me if you need anything," said Frieda kindly.

After thanking Frieda, the three all went together to wash and when they got back the stone table was set with a feast that would feed ten people. They all sat down excitedly to eat this amazing morning meal. Alli, Bade and Chief Tyee told Skye many stories of the capturing of Simon, saving his family, and the awful battle where Alli and Zenny had been injured. Bade was taking the last sips of his cocoa with disappointment on his face. Alli noticed and started to chuckle.

"I will make you some more warm cocoa later," she said, smiling.

"Bella sent something called hot chocolate bombs, one for each of us, if someone would heat four big cups of milk, we could have the special warm cocoa Bella sent," Skye said excitedly.

Bade instantly stood to go heat the milk and everyone laughed. Skye went to get her backpack from the door and retrieve the gifts. Bade returned a few minutes later carrying a tray of steaming cups with a stirring spoon in each one. Skye got out the bag from the chocolate shop and told the story of the wonderful smelling store. She opened the bag to find four balls, each in its own bag. She put them on the tray with the cups.

"Bella told me they have different flavours, either dark chocolate or orange cream. There are two of each kind."

Bade let Alli choose first, she chose a lighter colored one for herself and a dark colored one for Bade.

"Then we can share and try each flavor," she said, smiling at Bade. He kissed her cheek and passed out the other two. Chief Tyee chose the dark color and Skye chose the light color.

"Bella said just to drop them in hot milk and wait to be amazed," chuckled Skye.

The four of them dropped their bombs into the hot milk and watched. Chief Tyee's opened first, spilling delicious smelling liquid into his cup. The other three didn't have to wait long for their bombs to open and fill their cups with delicious cocoa too.

"Oooh how wonderful," said Alli as she tasted her warm cocoa.

Bade was gently stirring his cup to get the full effect of the bomb. He slowly took a sip, "This is really good; I will definitely need to thank Circee when I see her," said Bade.

Skye looked at Bade, "What do you mean when you see her?" Skye asked hopefully. Bade and Alli smiled at each other again.

"We have set our wedding date for six months from now and we are going to invite Circee to the wedding," said Alli excitedly.

"That is really great news," said Chief Tyee as he hugged his sister and then shook Bade's hand. I'm glad you two have set your date, I am looking forward to seeing you wed."

The group finished their delicious warm cocoa with stories from Skye about all the wonders she saw in Bella's world. Then Skye remembered the gift from Bella's mom and gave the package to Chief Tyee.

"This is for you from Bella's mom, she is a very brave warrior too. She was amazing and kept us safe from the scientist, who wanted to capture us and study us. Then she fearlessly got us back here without a hitch," said Skye reverently. Chief Tyee opened the silk drawstring gift bag and found a thank you note and the exquisite knife in its leather case. When Chief Tyee removed the knife from its case, he was surprised to see it was made from a similar thing to the arrows of his enemies.

"This material is very strong and sharp; Bella's mom must be a good craftsman. I would like to meet her. Can we invite her to the wedding with Bella?" asked Chief Tyee.

"That's a great idea," said Alli happily, "we will invite them both."

"Well enough merriment for me, I need to deal with the prisoners, I am going to have our guards walk them to the southernmost part of our land and set them free to go back to their home. I will also have given them a strong warning that if they return, they will be turned into mice. That should keep them away from our people and our dragons," chuckled Chief Tyee.

"I would like to go back to the keep and get to know the new babies," Skye said.

"Great idea Skye," affirmed Bade. "Can you take some of the morning meal leftovers to Simon and his family, please?"

Chief Tyee went to deal with the prisoners. Skye packed a tray for the newcomers and left to go to the keep. Bade cleaned up the meal while Alli rested on the couch dreaming of her wedding day.

Chapter 20

Happy Endings

Bella made it home and safely into the garage, she was worrying about her Mom and Skye. She wondered if the golden egg had hatched and if Zenny was okay after the battle. She was concerned for all of her friends, and it was making her mind a jumble of worry. She went into the house and got a drink of water and waited for Mom.

Mom returned an hour later and was carrying a big bag and a small box with holes in it. It was making a whimpering sound.

"Mom, I was so worried about you, what is that?" Bella stopped in her tracks, "no way, is that a pet?" she asked excitedly.

"Not just any pet," said Mom as she handed the box to Bella. Bella set the box down on the floor and sat down next to it. She opened the box with shaking hands and the very special puppy from the pet store poked its little head up from the box. Tears began to run down Bella's cheeks. This was the puppy she had wanted from the pet store.

"I think you have proven you are ready for a new puppy," said Mom proudly. "Skye told me you loved this little one."

"Thank you, Mom, he's perfect," said Bella. "Thank you, Mom, for everything you have done, You are my hero. I love you to the moon."

Bella hugged her Mom tightly and then they both sat down on the floor to play with their cute new puppy.

**Stay tuned for "Return to Crystal"
the third exciting adventure!**

9 789655 781762